"How wonderful that Robert ⎯⎯⎯, writer, dreamer, healer, and shaman, has decided to show us his soul! For decades he's encouraged us to find ourselves through our lucid dreaming, teaching us to fly, and to connect without fear with Spirit. Now, in his book of poems, *Here, Everything Is Dreaming,* which spans a 20-year period, he opens a window for us into his personal dreaming—and what a magical and multi-layered land it is. He shows us the pain and pleasure of a life lived fully, and the mysterious ways of the shamans that walk with us— if we are brave enough to see them. This is a book full of texture and wonder from a dreamer and poet in his prime."

—Candida Baker, author of *The Wisdom of Women: Intimate stories of love, loss and laughter*

"Through his haunting words and images, his 'shamanic songs for the seeker,' Robert Moss takes readers along on the soul's spiral journey through Life, Death, and The Return. He reminds us of ancient truths: 'Knowing is remembering;' 'The correct time is always now;' 'What you most fear is what you must do.' He beguiles us with stories of ancient myths existing in the midst of modern life. We meet the Great Bear, the Wise Man, the Fish, Silver Wolf, Red Fox, the Black Dog, Doubles, Ghosts of our future and past selves, and Guides. Moss urges us to find the grail 'in the one place it can be found'—ourselves. A rich gift for receptive readers."

— Patricia Garfield, author of *Creative Dreaming: Plan and Control Your Dreams to Develop Creativity, Overcome Fears, Solve Problems, and Create a Better Self*

"In *Here, Everything Is Dreaming*, Robert Moss, author, expert in shamanic practices and renowned founder of Active Dreaming, gathers a moving, enlightening, and beautifully crafted collection of fifty poems and ten short stories which taps into the recesses of our souls, brings us on a journey to the darkest parts of our consciousness, and back into the light.

Written between 1992 and 2012, Moss's luminous poems and stories (one might say parables) trace a path between the physical world, the world of myth and a world that exists in dreams. Entwining images from earth where the 'deer puts up antlers as taproots to the sky,' the elements 'from the place where fresh water joins the salt,' and love—carnal and spiritual—'The boy—or rather, what is working through him—has struck as deep as human teeth can go,' Moss remains fearless in his exploration of consciousness. What Moss has learned and what he brings back are Songlines, guideposts to fully-realized, integrated and poetic lives. Moss writes in one of his later poems, 'I did not leave *that* undone./I did not let my courage fail me./I did not obstruct water when it should flow.' May we rejoice in his vision."

— Joy E. Stocke, author of *Anatolian Days and Nights: A Love Affair with Turkey, Land of Dervishes, Goddesses, and Saints*

"Robert Moss has given us a phenomenal gift. His vivid collection of poems and stories, *Here, Everything Is Dreaming*, reveals the poet as a beguiling trickster who asks if we are 'asleep in the world, or awake in the dream?' He encourages us by example to travel off the map, to improvise, to seek the guidance of our dream soul in order to recover ourselves and be transformed. Moss moves effortlessly between worlds, spinning magical words that beckon beyond the edge of common perceptions where the mask of the ordinary falls away, revealing a primordial kinship with all that lives. He is a shapeshifter, practicing the primal art of regeneration, recognizing that to know is to remember what is most significant, then to act on it, again and again. This is, indeed, essential reading."

— Joan Marler, Executive Director of the
Institute of Archaeomythology

here, everything is dreaming

excelsior editions

AN IMPRINT OF STATE UNIVERSITY OF NEW YORK PRESS

HERE,
EVERYTHING IS DREAMING

poems and stories

ROBERT MOSS

Cover art: *The Dream of Pele*, by Caren Lobel-Fried ©
Photograph, page ii: *Provençal portal—Carcassonne*, by Robert Moss
Drawings by Robert Moss: *Pele Dreaming*, page iii; *Moon in My Room*, page 1;
Dreaming in Hawk, page 99
Photograph, page 169: Robert Moss with genie in Nîmes, by Irene Boulu
Photograph, page 170: Robert Moss opening a fire ceremony, by Jeanne Cameron

Published by
STATE UNIVERSITY OF NEW YORK PRESS, ALBANY

Printed in the United States of America

EXCELSIOR EDITIONS IS AN IMPRINT OF
STATE UNIVERSITY OF NEW YORK PRESS
For information, contact State University of New York Press, Albany, NY
www.sunypress.edu

Production and book design, Laurie Searl
Marketing, Kate McDonnell

LIBRARY OF CONGRESS CATALOGING-IN-PUBLICATION DATA

Moss, Robert, 1946–
Here, everything is dreaming : poems and stories / Robert Moss.
p. cm. — (Excelsior Editions)
ISBN 978-1-4384-4714-8 (pbk. : alk. paper)
I. Title.
PR6063.O83H47 2013
821'.914—dc23

2012029065

10 9 8 7 6 5 4 3 2 1

Contents

I SELECTED POEMS 1992—2012

Hunting Power   3

Chinaberry Gleam   4

A Flash of Blue   5

The Fire in the Wood   6

To the Deer of the Mountain   7

A Way of Creating   8

Rose Gate   9

Bear Giver   10

Scaffold Tree   12

The Return Journey   14

The Stand   17

Eldorado Kite   19

Praise for the Mother   20

Eyes of the Goddess   21

Birth of Apollo   23

Delivery Time   24

Bearing a Child from the Island of No Pain   25

Sun Stealer   28

White Wolf   30

Sunset Road   32

In Praise of Black Dogs   35

The Double on the Balcony   36

The Dragon's Plan   38

Angel of the Rushing Waters   39

The Art of Heronry   41

Rabbit at the Tree Gate   43

Bear Sightings   44

Brushes with the Red Fox   47

Glory Falls: On Harriet Tubman   49

I Dreamed I Woke Up   50

Beginner's Eyes, and After   52

Soul Is   54

A Crack in the House of God   55

If You Spill a Dragon   59

Moe'uhane: Island Dreaming   61

Lightning Paths   65

To the Blood Pool   67

Keepers of Time   69

Proteus   73

Becoming Caduceus   75

White Shadows   78

Night Calls   80

Kin to Lightning   82

Grail Knight   84

A Place to Write From (Red Ink)   86

Sanctuary   88

Wild Cherries   90

Anonwara: Turtle Dreaming   91

Because   92

Women Dream Dreams that would Terrify Men   94

Empathy Dreams   96

II TALES FROM THE IMAGINAL REALM

At the Gate of Story   101

Moon Tiger   106

The Xibalba Exchange   111

The Sign Language of the World   122

Love Tunnel   128

Unfinished Story   134

Flight to Deer Mountain   149

The Threefold Death of Silver Wolf   153

The Other, Again   157

The Journey to Absolute Knowledge   164

Acknowledgments   167

About the Author   169

PART I

SELECTED POEMS
1992—2012

HUNTING POWER

You say you are hunting your power,
but your power is hunting you.
I'll go up to the mountain, you say.
I'll fast and live on seaweed
I'll hang myself on a meathook
under the hot sun. I'll give up sex
and wine and my sense of humor.
What are you thinking of?
For you to go hunting your power
is as smart as the mouse hunting the cat.

Go out in the garden any night,
step one inch outside the tame land
and you are near what you seek.
Open the window of your soul
any night and your guide may come in.
The issue is whether you'll run away
when you see what it is. To make sure
you succeed, tether yourself like a goat
at the edge of the tiger wood that breathes
right beside your bed. He'll come.

—August 16, 2009

CHINABERRY GLEAM

Gentle soul, the Spirit caught you up as a raptor
beating wings, and tore your flesh
and drew you through the night worlds
and hurled you into deeps where no sun shines
and the moon is a blind pulse, a drum unheard,
so you would learn to shine in your own light
so you would steer by your inner sun
so you could unwrite the Book of Fate
so that, remembering, you move as a dancer among your kind,
in the world but not of it, not different and not the same,
sharing what you have lived at your heart's core:
love, and courage, the flash of the sea-horse racing waves,
the gleam of rain on a chinaberry tree.

—March 10, 1992

A FLASH OF BLUE

You see a flash of blue in the air at midnight,
that blue, the blue of kingfisher's wings,
and you take flight from the seen to the unseen.
Poor strategy: the unseen is my home.
You hide from me where I live.

—August 9, 1998

The Fire in the Wood

When you thought the fire was out,
flame leaps from the heart of the wood
so strong you're surprised it is safely contained
in what you supposed was a cold hearth.

There is nothing to warn you when it flares up.
Know this: tended or untended, the fire lives.
It will consume you. As fire lives in wood,
I live in you.

—August 9, 1998

To the Deer of the Mountain

—

Deepheart, mountain guardian
who harries the hunter
and knows what belongs to us
and what does not,
give us your speed,
your ability to read the land,
to see what is behind us and around us.

—

May we grow with the seasons
into your branching wisdom,
putting up antlers as taproots into the sky
to draw down the power of heaven,
reaching into the wounded places
to heal and make whole,
walking as living candelabra,
crowned with light,
crowning each other with light.

—November 6, 1999

A WAY OF CREATING

The buried city
bursts from the earth
as Van Gogh sunflowers.
The stem sustains the fruit.
This is a way of magic:
to write names of power
in the dust of the curio shop
and let them walk, ring doorbells
and instruct that old souls
inspire young ones, across time.

This is a way of begetting:
to turn in the cycle of creation,
to breathe clouds into the air,
colors into the fields,
and paint the sun into the sky.

—June 23, 2001

ROSE GATE

There's a garden among the stars
where flowers are gates to other worlds.
Try the pink rosebud that opens shyly,
plunge through its smooth and fragrant folds
into the Victorian garden where tea is laid
and sweet girls play and show a blushing priest
a bunny hole that leads to Wonderland
and a ginger cat issues opaque directions.

Take the dare of the "Drink Me" bottle
and you'll become inconceivably small
even faster than Alice, so fast you won't see
a grass blade rear into a royal palm
and ants turn into six-legged horses.

You'll grow, by diminishing, into a world
vaster than the one you knew before.
You'll swim among stars no telescope has seen,
you'll find light-ships among the galaxies,
immensity held in the iota of a speck
that eludes the electron microscope
but not the home-drawn voyager.

—July 8, 2001

BEAR GIVER

He walks with me like a faithful dog
though he's twice my size
and my ancestors feared and revered him so much
they never spoke his name out loud,
calling him Honey-mouth, or Sticky-paw,
or the Matchless One. Upright, he seems man
more than animal, though on cold nights
men in the wild would envy his fine warm pelt.

We are going to the animal doctor,
not the corner vet but the real thing,
because the Bear is ready to give himself again.
He passes without pain, without blood.
The animal doctor explains we must use all of him,
every organ, wasting nothing, sharing with those in need.

We unwrap the Great One as a medicine bundle.
Everything inside his skin is clean and dry,
sorted for use. The gall bladder is prized above all.
It will go to one who has earned it.
When we have used all of him, Bear is reborn,
the same Honey-mouth, in a new body.
The animal doctor says we must remember this always:

When you take from the Bear with respect, wasting nothing,
Bear always comes back, in a new pelt.

Now I walk with him in his new body
to help someone who has dreamed him,
padding softly down hospital halls.
The Master of Medicine gives himself over and over.
This is the most natural thing in the world.
There is no end to this, unless our love runs dry
and we forget what he is.

—July 9, 2001

SCAFFOLD TREE

From a dream photograph that might have been taken by A.L. Kroeber.

The pages of the talking book are thick
and floury to the touch. Blades of shadow
in the old black-and-white plates cut
Klamath landscapes into sourbread slices.
The tree in the photo that draws me
spreads stocky bare limbs from a headland.
Dark eagles roost, row on row.
Two women perch among them, second row
on the right. Can this be a group portrait?
The tree stands like a scaffold.

I must know more. I lean into the picture
and find it is an open window.
Leaning through, I see the tree has no roots;
strong native men hold it in place,
tensing their muscles against the wind
that wants to sweep it out across the bay.
Everything has been prepared by man's—
or woman's—intention. Birds and women
perch on cross-boughs tied together.
Early ethnographers, Teutonic ladies

of military mien, stand bespectacled watch
but will not speak to the interloper at the window.

I turn back to the book for help.
On the facing page is a Farewell Song.
The book sings utterly foreign words to me
full of long Es, full of keening,
and counsels me never to confuse
a terminal N with a final M.

I think this would be a sweet way to go:
to leave the body in the scaffold tree
to be picked clean by fastidious carrion birds.
Better than moldering in the earth
or, viler still, in an airtight cask above it.
I will have my body burned to white ash
when my spirit is done with it
because scaffold trees are problematic
in places with health codes and too many people.
Yet in my heart I would like to fly off
with the sea-going eagles, rising into beauty.

—*July 9, 2001*

The Return Journey

You found the courage
to turn on the tiger who pursued you
to fight with him hand to claw
to be swallowed and spat out
and to win through your losing
reforged in a shining body
worthy now to take his heart
and call him as your unswerving ally.
   It is not enough.

Out of your yearning
you danced into worlds of enchantment
you drank from the breasts of the Goddess
where kisses flower into hyacinths
caresses stream into rivers of milk
every nerve ending is a partner in love
and hearts are never broken.
You discovered that dreaming is magic.
   But it's not enough.

As a confident traveler, you learned
to shrug off your bodyshirt
and ride the World Tree
as your private elevator

to soar through the face of the moon
dance with the Bear among the stars
to enter the sun behind the sun
and fly on wings of paradise over a fresh world.
You're out there, but it's not enough.

Out of your calling
you braved the gates of the Underworld
and crossed the borderless river on your heartbeat
and tricked the Dark Angel in his own realm.
When you stood, defeated, before the impregnable walls
of Death itself, you raised a song from your heart and belly
that called help from the highest heaven
to pluck a soul from the cold recreation yard
where nobody plays new games.
But you must make the return journey.

The way back is full of diversions.
Some will detain you with pink kisses;
some will drag on you as drowning men.
You'll find the markers have been moved, or stolen.
Maybe you'll have gone so deep, or so high,
you can't remember which world you left your body in.
Or you'll rebel against returning to a world
where hearts are broken, and the earth defiled.
You will return. This is your soul's agreement.

Now you have danced with the Bear
you will bring healing to the world of pain.
Now you have traveled the roads of soul
you will help the soul-lost to bring their children home.
Now you have flown as Apollo on a shining arrow
you will bring light into the shadow world.
Now you know the gates and paths of the Real World
you will make bridges for others.

You will bring it all home.

Returning, you will remember your mission:
To serve the soul's remembering;
to go among people as dream ambassador
opening ways for soul to be heard and honored.
Let the world be your playground, not your prison.
Starchild, plunge with delight into the warm, loamy earth,
renew the marriage of Earth and Sky,
follow your heart-light, dance your dreams,
commit poetry every day, in every way.

Now you are home.

—July 20, 2001

The Stand

The erotic scent of wood's decay and earth after rain
fills the primal stand of giant poplars, oaks and elms
and I know I have been coming here always.
The golden one parts the forest as a wing of light.
The dark one pushes through as a ruthless red boar.
They come without armies, without banners,
though legions have bled for them, and empires died.
They meet as She who watches loves them best:
as lithe young men in their prime of manhood,
as antlered kings in the fierce season, fighting to possess.

There has never been peace between them,
only a balance that shifts and spills, never still or sure.
They battle now with the arms of the forest,
wielding uprooted trees as spears, as clubs.
The trees groan and sway, taking sides.
The golden one finds the opening for the killing blow
but stays his hand. From his hesitation, the dark king
gains boldness and vigor, and drives a rowan
deep into his brother's side. Wounded and waning,
the light king drags himself to the mothering oak
and darkness swallows the sun. The dark one
raises a cry that calls hungry ghosts to the feast.

But something restrains him from the final act.
It can only be Her voice, walking through his mind.

If either wins, the game is over.
Without contraries, nothing is created.
It is through your unending battle
and its lack of resolution
that the game goes on.

The dark one brings a gift to the wounded king.
A flock of seven black sheep. One of them gags
and vomits up a glowing blue egg.
With his last strength, the light twin palms the gift
and his body is suffused with healing light.
He rises, intact, ready to renew the battle
here, or anywhere that is world.

—August 4, 2001

ELDORADO KITE

The great bird lifts from my hand
drawn to the sun
on Your breath.
I tug on the string,
trying to drag it down,
forgetting what You taught me:
the falcon longs for the wrist of the King.

This strange wind is too strong for me.
I am rising with the bird
above all that is fenced in,
urgent to cut the cord.
My tame self panics.
It wants to hide among limits and shadows
where air does not move like *this*,
in animate waves of intent.

Something falls like a worn-out coat
and Your breath blows me as a sail
across oceans of sky
to my home in Your heart
where falcon and falconer are one.

—January 22, 2002

PRAISE FOR THE MOTHER

I am walking with the Mother.
I am sailing on her skin.
I become her child and lover,
from the outside enter in.

I will praise the sky above her.
I will praise her in the deep.
I am dreaming with the Mother.
She awakens me from sleep.

Walk lightly on the Mother
and let her grace unfold.
Praise and serve the Mother
and re-enchant the world.

Praise and serve the Mother
and re-enchant the world.

—*December 4, 2002*

Eyes of the Goddess

The poet waits for me in his countryman's cape
and shows me the map in the gateway stone:
twin spirals to get you in, and out, of the place of bone;
wave paths to swim you from shadow to dreamscape;
a stairway of stars for when you are done with earthing.
I am here to practice the art of rebirthing.

She calls me, into the belly of the land that is She.
But I play, like the poet, with the shapes of time:
I am a swimming swan on the River Boyne;
I am a salmon, full with the knowing of the hazel tree;
I wander with Angus, and know the girl I have visioned
in gold at the throat of a white swan, beating pinions.

Drawn by the old perfume of burned bones, I go down
and doze until solstice fire, bright and bountiful,
quickens me for the return of the Lady, lithe and beautiful
in the form she has taken, flowing as liquid bronze.
Her face is veiled, so the man-boy called to her side
like the red deer in season will not die in her eyes.

I see beyond the veil, for I come from the Other.
Oh, I yearn for the smell of earth and the kiss of rain!

I leap with her on the hallowed bed, coming again.
She knows the deer-king, as I am child and lover.
Her eyes are spiral paths; the gyre of creation whirls
and sends me in green beauty to marry the worlds.

—*December 18, 2002*

BIRTH OF APOLLO

I cannot be born
on solid ground,
only where everything flows.
To enter my dawn
you must be unbound
from how the fixed world goes.

Leave behind
your maps and losses,
let dreams be all your law.
Trust the wind
when the ocean tosses;
burn your boats on the farther shore.

Make new songs
and your floating island
will be rooted beneath the waves.
Drink my sun
and you dance on the high land
your heart, remembering, craves.

—December 20, 2002

DELIVERY TIME

Slick with blood, shiny with fluid,

the stag is born fully formed,

testing his hooves and horns.

He comes from me whole and magnificent.

I am giddy with delight and bear no scar.

I do not know how he came out

until his great chest breaks open

like a two-leaved cabinet

and he births from his own being

the one who completes him.

Slick with fluid, shiny with blood,

the deer mother comes heavy with child,

ready to deliver in the usual way.

—December 31, 2002

Bearing a Child from the Island of No Pain

There is an island beyond pain,
friendly to magic, where children sing
and delight in learning the necessary things:
the language of birds, how wishing is doing,
how to walk on moonlight and swim in the rain.

To get there, you must go off the maps,
track what rhymes in a day, do magical passes
and go to Raven, Madrona and Orca for remedial classes
in wearing darkness lightly, shedding old skin
and plunging deep. You must travel through the gaps

in the obvious world. The island reaches to you—
how else could you know it?—in your dreams.
One morning you fall awake with the gleam
of memory of a wise child, whole and beautiful,
who owns herself but is gone from you.

You long to go through the mist where she has gone,
to dance with shamans who heal to entertain
and there is no fear, betrayal or shame.
The red fingers of the tree that binds the shore
tap in madrona code: "Go, and bring her home."

You are off in a heartbeat, a sail unfurled.
Your dream soul is your leader
to the house of rain and red cedar
where the lovely child flees from you;
she won't live in your body, won't breathe in your world.

You will lose her again. Except for the great white Bear
who comes to embrace and enfold you
both, and will not let go, but holds you
together, till you cannot pull apart.
In the arms of Bear Mother, the unhealed tear

in your being opens the door to your heart
and your child comes in, suspicious of your vows—
"We'll have fun!" "What's ours is ours."
"I'll never let them hurt you."
"I'll stand in my power." "We'll never be apart."

Your double scream of birthing
scares the gentle black-tailed deer
from the orchard, and sows fear
of miscarriage. But the Bear is with you
and in you, bringing you to a place of birthing.

You drink apple juice from the tree
and your soul swells and claps her hands.

The wise child looks out of your eyes and understands you will live your promises, be shaman of your self, call souls back in others. You are home, and free.

—August 30, 2005

SUN STEALER

They say you stole the sun.
This is inexact.
You hid the light in darkness
where the light-killers could not find it
so the sun could shine brighter than before.

They say you are black
because you are evil and unkind.
They do not say you swallowed
your own shadow and mastered it
at the price of wearing its color.

Shivering, they call you death-knell,
death-eater, bad omen, flying banshee,
because you feed on death that feeds on men.
You strip what rots from what remains.
You give us the purity of the bones.

Trickster, they call you.
Oh yes, you'll do your wickedest
to ensure our way is never routine
and we are forced to improvise and transform.
You won't let us swap our souls for a plan.

At least they don't accuse you
of minor crimes.

I praise and claim your gifts
of putting on darkness to come and go safely
in the darkest places, and joking with Death.

—September 11, 2005

WHITE WOLF

Mother of wolves,
hunter of hearts,
you are the antidote
to the wolf in man.

Never tame,
you gentle our wildness.
You help us turn packs
into families.

Killer of fear,
cleanser of souls,
you shear away
what is dead, or meant to die.

You bring light from dark;
on the night your scary twin
eats the moon,
you give us white fire.

On your bicycling legs,
with your flawless compass,
you take us into the shining heart
of the Peacemaker.

Over the black rubble
of our guilt and shame
you spread a clean mantle
of fresh-fallen snow.

Your clear eyes read
what belongs to us and what does not;
you know better than we do
what it takes to be human.

—*May 26, 2006*

SUNSET ROAD

I

A piece of sky has fallen into the sea,
so this must be the time.
The Sound is banded pink and heron blue
by the gentle palette of the lowering sun.

I strip at the shore of the shelly beach
and fold my clothes neat as Christmas packages.
I was never tidy in life, except in leaving it,
so they'll know that I left with intention.

The water receives me in a lover's embrace.
Discreetly, the watcher on the reef takes off
and becomes a black arrow, flying west,
beyond the lighthouse island, pointing my way.

There has been a sea-change; the chop and current
that resisted me fiercely, day after day,
pushing me always toward the Old World,
now streams with my strokes.

I am riding blue water, crested with burning bronze.
How my body loves the sea, its element and its nature!

I swim through all the colors of memory
and I remember the water-world that is my home.

Something slips from me like a swimsuit
whose elastic has snapped, and I am free of human form.
I am a cormorant, fishing and skimming the waves.
I play with the shapes I remember:

I am a dolphin, leaping and plunging in its joy.
I am a sea-king in his chariot, plowing the waves.
I am the Blue Man, tireless lover from the deep.
I am the one who fell from the sky like a shooting star.

II

I remember the sunset road. Perhaps I looked too long
into the black light at the heart of the sun
because I have skipped a continent, and return to myself
on the white sand of Manly Beach.

For a moment, I am in the body and memory
of an awkward Australian boy of eighteen
learning how to make love. Quickly I am drawn
through green shadows and groves of familiar dead

to the World Tree. It has an everyday name:
Moreton Bay fig. The flocks of ibis birds around it—

travelers from the precinct of Thoth, the star voyager,
measurer and rememberer—herald its greater name.

Its corkscrew roots drill a passage to the Underworld.
Its manifold trunks and branches open many ways.
Its upper limbs are ladders to the World Up Top,
where a couple with black opal eyes help me up.

In the lubra's opulent body I read a pattern of stars.
Her eyes shift. She is flying fox, and echidna,
and black Venus. Her eyes turn as spiral galaxies,
and I find she is a way through the Milky Way.

—September 22, 2006

IN PRAISE OF BLACK DOGS

I am in favor of personal superstitions;
not the kind Granma mumbles
or the stuff of fright-night movies,
but the ones that grow on you
when you notice which incidents in a day
are shadows cast by something ahead
and get to know which clues from the world
are reliable road signs.

I think a black dog, if friendly,
is always a good omen
and could be a god traveling in disguise.
Some days you don't have to figure this out.
At the door of possibility on San Francisco Bay
a black dog crossed my path.
His walker, a ruddy man in a red pixie hat,
told me the dog's name is Pollo,
short for Apollo.
I have a black dog of my own.
His name is Nubie, short for Anubis.
He lives in my dreams
and takes on many bodies in the world.

—*October 22, 2006*

THE DOUBLE ON THE BALCONY

You are not my shadow.
You stand closer to the sun.
Of all my doubles, you are the most interesting.
You are watching when I forget you.
You are with me when I don't notice.
You are not my judge, or my guardian angel.
You are the one who remembers.
You are my witness on the balcony above the world.

My friend the witch doctor calls you
my "double in heaven." You smile at this,
reminding me the African lives are mine, not yours.
You saw all of it, from your balcony,
but did not drink the blood or savage joy.
It's the other way round in other lives, you say;
from life to life, we change places.
When you come down to earth,
I take your seat on the terrace above.

We are together now, for a moment.
I've slipped out of the body
that neither confines nor delights you
to join you on your balcony above the world.

The wine in the cup is the color of moonlight.
Below us are all the roads of the world,
the casts and dramas of the many lives
laid out in dioramas, as manageable from here
as toy soldier sets, or tea-party dolls.

You chide me gently (since humans are forgetful animals)
for forgetting you. I have been a serial amnesiac,
losing bright nights when we roamed together,
and an ingrate—not seeing your hand in everyday miracles,
not hearing your voice in the still sure moments of knowing,
not feeling the breeze of your wing when you come,
in reluctant extremity, to restrain or release me.

When my road was blocked, you were the one
who reminded me we can fly.
You love to travel in disguise,
and I often missed you behind your masks.
When I mislaid my sense of humor,
you burst in as a stand-up comic
and shocked me alive with belly-bawdy farce.
It's easy for you to bring light, and lighten things up;
you stand closer to the sun.

—*October 29, 2006*

The Dragon's Plan

I'll kill you first,
then we'll see whether
there's anything useful
to be done with you.
Does that sound like a plan?

We'll wrap you in shrouds;
you'll stiffen before you deliquesce
and give up your bones.
My heartbeat will call you
to rise in a greater body.

This is the Dragon way:
I kill what is small and safe in you
to birth the awaited one
with sinews of spring fire
who lifts a cry that wakes the gods
and brings them back
into the game of the world.

—February 19, 2007

Angel of the Rushing Waters

I have seen you as a purple bruise in a yellow sky,
as a Scottish soldier with drawn sword
at the edge of the tame land and the wild wood,
as a snowy owl with fierce talons and fiercer eyes,
as an Indian death-lord traveling abroad
in a Johnny Cash outfit, swinging a lasso.

I have felt you enter as a gentle breeze
stirring the curtains of a window in a hospital room,
and in the raw, thrusting horsepower
of the dark lord bursting into the sunlit maiden meadow.

You are a sexy devil.
I love you better than your brother Sleep.
Through aching nights of absence
I have longed for your embrace.

I have run your errands,
speaking in your voice to the old golfer on the plane,
negotiating with your razor-sharp precision
the terms for a possible life extension.
I have taken ailing humans by the hand
to your deep pools, to find you—if they dare—
in the troubling of the waters.

Few can look into your black sun,
but those who do are different.
To know you, to walk with you,
to feel you always at the left shoulder
brings courage and October light.

You love to dress for occasions.
I have encountered you as a dandy in evening dress,
as a red Irish big-bellied god, and an Indian flame,
and a white lady whose footsteps are frost.
Your image is rarely in public places
though the medieval mind, like the mind of Mexico,
puts skeletal reminders of you at every turning,
mocking the vanities of the world.

On our wedding day
I want you to reach down from the sky in your robe of stars
and catch me in your voluptuous embrace
as we leave my old garment in the blanket of earth.
But if you choose not to come in your goddess form,
I want you to be wearing my face.

—April 29, 2007

THE ART OF HERONRY

I am studying your art.

You are a master of patience.

You can wait on one leg,
a spearman poised and immobile,
longer than I can wait on two (or three).
Your standing stillness cons the fish
into disregarding you, as a dead branch
or a boring relic from an old shipwreck.

You don't need anyone to tell you
when the time is Go.
In that instant, you strike without delay,
your purpose straight and swift and clean
as a stabbing spear, taking your prey.

I am relieved that even you
have to work to get airborne,
flapping and beating your gray-blue wings.
When you are up, and stretch out your body,
you exhibit the whole history of flight.
You show yourself as the Feathered Serpent,
the one that grew wise enough
to make a home in another dimension.

I love the way you practice love.
You put on a gaudy show for your intended,
sprouting twin mating plumes.
When your gallantry prospers,
you are willing to work in intimate partnership.
I have seen you ferrying twigs in your beak
to your mate in the frame of your nest in the tree.

High-flying bird of the heart,
I like your business arrangement
with the busy engineer of canals and dams;
where the beaver builds, you build too.

Humans, who fly only in dreams and machines,
know you as an ancient ally and exemplar.
You brought First Woman from the earth in the sky,
breaking her fall on wings spread like magic carpets,
to dance a new earth into being.

Egypt knows you, and the mystery of your rise
from the sexy serpent of earth
to the master of air and of water.
Egypt calls you the ever living, the bennu bird,
born again and again from the ashes of the old life,
endlessly birthing your winged and shining self.

—June 6, 2007

RABBIT AT THE TREE GATE

The glint of gold in the rabbit's eye
is the reflection of the hawk's fierce gaze.
Seer of the sky, master of wind,
forever poised to kill the timid bunny self,
he allows only one avenue of escape:
Alice's way, down the rabbit hole
into a world beneath the world we know.

A branch creaks in the wind like a door;
acorns clack like dice among the roots.
You will go down, again and again,
until you make peace with the ancestors
and earn the blessing of the Mother.

Then, but not before, you may ask
what you can know as absolute knowledge—
the truth of sunlight refracted by lake water,
the love of an innocent child,
the face of the one you will always love,
wading birds on a cold Scottish coast—
and grow green again, in the eye of the hawk.

—June 16, 2007

BEAR SIGHTINGS

You stood in the middle of a country road
to make me stop and listen.
I got round you and said, when my heart slowed,
that a bear in the road is just coincidence.

So you came over in the middle of the night
and stood between me and the moonlight
and scared me so bad with your size and the surprise,
I jumped out of my skin.

A fox barked in the woods and snickered,
"What are you thinking of?
In your body or out of it,
you are now in the dream of the Bear."

So when you came again, taller than my ceiling,
I made myself enter your embrace.
I thought I would die in your arms;
instead, I grew to your size, and we danced.

You showed me we are joined at the heart
as an unborn child is joined to its mother
by a thick umbilical pumping life juice.
You told me to call on you for healing.

There are days when I still forget you.
One night, from a hilltop, I saw you on the road
like a walking mountain, dwarfing the cars.
I feared you would crush them like matchbox toys.

Fox barked again, and I saw you were the shadow
thrown by the moonlight from my shoulders.
I had not known your power with me had grown so big,
and that I must choose whether it will harm or heal.

I am still remembering you. I remember now
that I knew you when I was a soldier in leather armor
fighting under the banner of the Bear Goddess.
Weary, I went to die in wild country, but you healed me.

I remember that when the Real People laid my body
in the blanket of Mother Earth, I found rest
in the heartwood of an oak until, stirring from my long nap,
I sought life in a newborn cub that could fit in a pink palm.

You are healing. I have seen you open yourself
as a medicine chest, offering all you contain.
You are protection. I have seen you gather your kind
to form an unbreakable circle of defense against the dark.

Behind all your forms, you are the Mother.
You made me find the right song

to open a door in the roots of the Life Tree
and receive your blessing in a world beneath the world.

I bring others here, to be nursed and healed
in your generous lap, and be joined to their dream selves,
their wonder-children, their powers of healing and creation—
that fled from them when they fled from you.

—June 23, 2007

BRUSHES WITH THE RED FOX

I blamed the demon mist for turning me around
and making an island where there was none before
and hiding my way on a road I know well,
until the curtain of fog was pulled back
and there you were, trotting ahead on my left side.
You live on the edges of my life
at the margin of the tame land and the wild
and your appearances are always edgy for me.

You are a determined messenger.
Once you got into my throat and choked me
near to death, like a chunk of charred oat bread
rammed down the gullet of a druid sacrifice.
I know the one: he was fished out of a bog
in the old country, wearing a bracelet of your fur.
He died the triple death, coughing up his spirit
to intercede with the gods of above and below.
I never wanted to be him. . . . But
you taught me the reasons for sacrifice.

You know when to hide and when to hunt.
Men chase you on horseback, with dogs,
yet turn chicken when you turn up unannounced.

You are tricky. I doubt I'll ever be at ease with you.
Yet you are a necessary link to old and sacred things
and you call women I care for to reclaim lost soul
and become fabulous Foxy Girls, immune to glass ceilings,
setting their own boundaries, living unbounded life.

—July 18, 2007

Glory Falls: On Harriet Tubman

Because you could fly,
you made us stand up and walk
and become self-liberators,
even when fear tore at our souls
rougher than the spikes of the gum nuts,
winter's nail bed of pain.
You rode the wind on hawk wings
and saw roads out of the shadow lands
and made maps for us from your flights.

When we were too scared to trust you,
you sang courage back into our hearts.
You guided us through the night woods
on leopard feet, vanishing and reappearing,
never bound to one form. Through your pain
and sudden sleeps and the terrible wound
that branded you, you taught us
that gifts of greatness are in our wounds.
You led us into the province of wonder.
The engine of your fierce intent carried us
to where glory falls on every thing.

—March 7, 2008

I Dreamed I Woke Up

I dreamed I woke up.
In this waking life my thoughts
are agate points and deep lagoons
that make ancient cities and heroes
and bust dakinis out of lunch boxes.

Everything is alive when I am awake.
I remember to swim in air
and fly in water, and ride moon tigers
to the Moon Cafe, and the light in my head
is the light of the blue-white star.

I went back to sleep in a world
of fewer voices and more noise. Out here
in mossy woods, sleep life is pleasant.
It's good to watch a cedar shake her frills,
good to be surprised by lime on watermelon.

There are days I don't want to wake up.
Then there are days of pain and lost delight,
city days caught in time and trivial stories
when I forget that I am asleep
and can change the game if I awaken.

I cannot say whether the person writing this is asleep in the world, or awake in the dream.

BEGINNER'S EYES, AND AFTER

I

I'm in no hurry to open my eyes
in the delivery room in this embodied world.
I linger in breathing dark against the woman's skin,
remembering the amniotic lake
and the high windy spaces before it
where I traveled in a cloak lined with stars.
I raise the eyelid curtain reluctantly.
I do not find my blue memories among these pink faces,
but I discover lacy greens beyond a barred window.
The bars can't be strong enough to hold a traveler,
and the skylight looks like a way home.

II

After many years in this body, past the midpoint
for life in this form, the bars are thicker.
Sometimes I can't see beyond them, and I forget
there is a hole in this world that opens into the sky
and I am lost to the story that brought me here.
Then my friend comes to remind me, sailing on flat wings.
His shadow is like a stealth bomber or an angel.
His fierce intent rips me from the consensual daze

through lightning storms and battles of crazy gods
to the clear blue depth where I recover myself
and can study the human drama as a manageable diorama.
The tiny players are easy to move and hard to take seriously.

When you lose beginner's eyes, you need eagle eyes
to regain the world behind the world, and the deeper story.

—August 15, 2008

SOUL IS

The soul is something that is always trying to leave,
like a caged bird longing for the sky.
To keep it in my heart,
I must spread the wings of life
and let the sun rise within me every day
and fly from the skeleton beach over the whitecaps
drinking wind, and let my body love what it loves
and remember what I forget
when my nights are filled by your absence:
this world is my playground, not my prison.

—*October 12, 2008*

A CRACK IN THE HOUSE OF GOD

"Ma tu perché vai?"

"Per tornar altra volta la dov'io son."

—Dante, Purgatorio II 90–92

They call this city the House of God
in a language no one here can speak.
I came to it along a roadkill highway
where only the red fox passed, unscathed,
before my car, cackling a message I couldn't catch.
The gatekeeper at the inn is unfriendly.
Squat as a toad behind his transparent shield,
he snaps and swallows cash and credit
but still won't unlock the lobby door.
He sends me round by the left-hand path
past the dry pool and cupids whose arrows never flew
and a solitary white swan on a dark pond
bereft of her mate and her own graceful kind.

We are going to dine in a city of the East
and we have a flawless navigator, talking
over moving pictures, dinging approval
when we turn as we are told. But we don't know
the state of being where our hunger will be fed,

so we quarrel with the guide and with each other
until we enter a different state. We turn and turn again
until we are back at the place from which we started
and know our way for the first time.
Directions are no use unless you know your destination.
Late for dinner, we are met by an antlered doorman.
There is a lion on my "Drink-Me" bottle.
I swallow deep, and the red fox jumps up
from the shadows, mouthing the word "Hellblazer."

Back at the inn, my room reeks of sulfur,
as if I never left the place from which I surely ascended.
I check my guidebook—when in doubt,
consult a dead poet, as Beatrice called Virgil for Dante.
The guidebook explains that we travel to return
to where we are. Yes, this could be the right place;
there are directions to a gate you can easily miss
because it first appears as the merest crack in a wall.
But when you brave the steps, and knock on your heart,
it roars louder than myth, and opens a way to the stars.

In the prime time of birth and death, still far from dawn,
the stillness explodes into the crashing of doors
and a wild clamor of voices, and my neighbors' room
turns into a rave party, or a crack house.
I give them an hour to quiet down,

but this isn't that kind of crowd,
so I put on my leather armor to reclaim the night.

Outside, I am drawn to the black pond and the white swan
who turns with hieratic grace at the midpoint.
When I walk down to the water's edge,
she glides to me at once, so close I can touch her breast.
Her great wings, folded, make the shape of a heart.
When I try to read her dark and shining eyes,
I see the sadness of a lovely woman in white,
and in her eyes, mirrors within mirrors,
I find a blazing phoenix fire of many colors
and know this is reflected glory of the heaven bird
who flies fearless through all the worlds.
"Where is your mate?" I ask the white swan.
Words swim back. *How long have you made me wait?*
And: *How many dreams of me did you forget?*
How many signs from me did you refuse?
I can only answer with truth: "I have been a fool,
silly and forgetful, but I have always loved you."

I remember a blessing of my ancestors:
"Dark is the city. Dark are those who live there.
You are the white swan going down among them.
No word of theirs may harm you.
Their tongue is under your foot."

In my leather armor, I raid the drug party.
Knives flash in the eyes of a razor girl,
but they go softly. Car doors clash, then silence.

I sit down to write in the gray dawn, when the poet says
mind is farther from the flesh and less trapped in thoughts.
The banker's lamp on the desk is broken,
proving it's for real, since banks are broken too.
Then I take the road past the house of the card-reader
who sometimes finds the Hanged Man and often the Fool,
and I remember that on this road, in the state
of Connecticut mind, they drowned Jerusalem
in a man-made lake to drive pleasure boats over the dead.

—October 5, 2008

IF YOU SPILL A DRAGON

If you spill a dragon,

    don't think about washing the tablecloth.

Everything interesting happens on the boundaries,

and when you are real, shabbiness doesn't matter.

You can't see the whole picture when you're in it,

and inside the soft animal of your body, you forget

that you are a star that came down because

    you wanted a messier kind of love.

Everyone has their own sky and their own trail

Directions only work if you know where you're going.

Instead of maps, use clues falling through the curtain

    of your constructed world.

A dream is a clickable link to the multiverse.

Horses always know who's really in charge.

Blackbirds speak truth and there are grandmothers

    wherever you look.

Follow your heart-light but wear a mirror on your back.

Check your crystal ball for malingering imps

and watch out for the Emperor of Enchantments

who traps lost souls in palaces of illusion.

What you most fear is what you most need to do.
Shake coincidence on drab days like quick curry sauce.
When the dragon cracks the wineglass of your life,
   flaunt the biggest stain as your banner.

—*November 16, 2008*

MOE'UHANE: ISLAND DREAMING

Dreaming is when soul wakes up
and goes traveling.
You may fly across the water
in your body of wind
following the drumming of the waves
to spend the night with your dream lover.
Even goddesses do this.

Pele left her lava bed for three days
to make love with her dream prince.
Being a goddess, she could bring him home.
It's harder for humans. Spend too long
with your dream spouse
without bringing him home
and you sicken like rotting silver.

You need to check who you're sleeping with
because spirits take many forms.
If your prince is a water imp in disguise,
you'll go fish belly white and moist
on the side that rests next to him.

You must learn the vocabulary of dreams.
Never confuse a wild goatfish dream

that begins and ends in your belly
with a dream that comes true
because it's the memory of a trip to the future.
Don't mix up a wishing dream with revelation.

Be alert to the visions that open and shut
like lobster pots, quick and true,
on the edges of sleep and waking.
Use the dreams that are given to heal a family
and dreams that show you how to heal yourself.

In beauty and terror, as redbirds or lovely sharks,
as windflowers or razorbacks or honeycreepers,
gods and ancestors are talking, talking.
They show us life's hidden springs.
They compose songs in us. They give
night names for babies that are coming.
They save our skins when they are worth saving.

Learn to discern when you can sweeten a dream
and soften the sharp future it portends
and when you have to swallow it straight up.
For a second opinion, listen to the birds
or to a bird-man who talks to the wind
or might sail a blossom canoe for you
over submarine tattoos in a gourd filled with water.

In the islands, everything has a body of wind.
In the morning garden, you notice the pandanus
has walked to the far side of the pond
where the fish dream open-eyed;
a palm swapped places with an avenging angel.
Even the land snail goes flying at night
and is the preferred scout of the fiercest goddess.

To become a native of these islands,
you must grow double vision, reading signs
in the world and the world-behind-the-world
without going crazy. Persevere
and all your dramas will lead
to the Place of Leaping,
where fresh water meets salt water,
and you'll drop your old body
and travel on, as bird or fish or zephyr,
to the land tourists never see on the horizon.

Here, everything is dreaming.
On a white beach in the early light
a shark came out of the waters
and became a graceful silver woman
who claimed me as her mate,
there on the embracing sand.
She was so lovely I was not put off

by her hammerhead eyes.

I wonder what unexplainable love child

is swimming out there, in the deep.

—*November 23, 2008*

LIGHTNING PATHS

Before lightning strikes,
feeders unseen by the ordinary I
travel possible paths through the air
to find the right way to bolt to earth.
Before the secret green cells in the leaf
drink from its suncatchers, light walks
all paths through the protein scaffold.

Scientists say that any road taken
collapses all possible paths.
In the leaf, in the air, in a human span
no road, perhaps, is entirely untaken.

If our lives are gardens of forking paths,
what happens when we take one branch
with the definite body? Do possible selves
travel on along all the possible paths?
Can we meet each other?
Can the branching paths rejoin?

In default mode I departed a mental map
and followed a road I thought I had left
toward an old place. When I saw my error,
I thought at least I was on familiar ground

on my ghost trail. I bulled across many lanes
to make an utterly wrong turn and did not see
I was speeding the wrong way on the Royal Road
until I met a familiar, a bull on a steakhouse sign.
It's not so easy to get back on a road you left.

To get my head around this
I'll go on a quantum walk tonight.
Like light in the leaf, like lightning's feeders,
we try all paths in our dreams.
When we are witness to ourselves,
we can change the default mode
and weave the many roads into the right one.

—January 28, 2009

To the Blood Pool

In the green garden of the heart
a lusty sea god fountains in a bronze surf
of mermaids. Bluebells are out
under the tender green canopy of the beeches.
A bee is unscrolling a hibiscus under a wall
and lavender fields beyond the far terraces
tempt me with their perfumes.

I answer the call of horses drilled for dressage;
they are prancing in place under the bridle.
In powder-blue coat and tight peruke
I mount my favorite creamy mare and ride her
round and round the great ellipse until it is time
to leave the grounds of the winter palace
for wilder places. I fly up stone-cut stairways
to a cobbled street that smells of oranges
and find myself, at last, at the blood pool.

I did not know it until I came here.
The blood in the round pool is fresh,
flowing from a secret spring. Seeking its source
I see the faces of those I have loved and lost
and unhealed wounds and interrupted dreams.

A black dog comes to guide me,

walking on my right. A lion flanks me on the left.

They bring me to the Antlered One.

He glows like electrum and between his horns

sun and moon float together.

How could I have forgotten him?

Blood flows unceasingly from his great heart,

freely and unobstructed, into the red pool,

where it is thinned as a painter thins his oils.

Here the lion laps courage. Here I dip

my pen in the inkwell of the heart

and find regeneration in the ever-giving wound.

—*March 1, 2009*

KEEPERS OF TIME

I

THE STRAPLESS WATCH

The correct time is always now
except when the time is GO.
All time, past and present,
is accessible in the moment
of this realization, and may be changed.

Yet within the spacious Now,
the Keepers of Time sometimes require
more specifics. On temporal assignment
to a war-torn country, skipping back decades,
I carry a strapless watch in my pocket.
At the perimeter of my landing place
female guards check new arrivals
to make sure they have the right time.
A pretty woman in Air Force blue
smiles at the watch face I hold up
between thumb and forefinger, clearing me
to explore a past that is now my future.

The House of Time is the Grand Central
of my transtemporal expeditions.
The gatekeeper is often friendly,
content to try out invited visitors
with the usual question (What is the time?)
and to accept the usual answer of the awakened.
Yet today, at the steps of the House of Time,
rising ziggurat-vast between great silver beaks,
is a different Keeper. He is living stone,
with four wings and four crowned heads,
and on his breastplate, endlessly revolving,
a disk with four arms resembling hourglasses,
tokens of time and infinity. This time my passport
is a symbol of unstrapped time, a lemniscate
I fit to the groove in the Keeper's breastplate.

He becomes the door through which I enter
a savage world unasked-for yet familiar,
the world of the Chaldean Time Lord
who lives all at once in four eras: his own
time of hanging gardens and jealous kings,
known to Daniel; the heyday of Assyria;
and that of princes of Persia who followed

mysterious Zurvan, god of Time-behind-time;
and an epoch when humanity's teachers
rose from the depths of ocean on the astral tides.
The Chaldean, sensing my presence,
is not welcoming. He prefers to dream my life
rather than have me dreaming his. I leave him
calibrating the mesh of his four ancient selves
and repair to the Library of Time to seek
information in its book-lined calm.

At the door of the Mesopotamian Room—
I see its winged bulls and lions, human-headed—
the librarian intercedes to direct me
to "a gentleman who can help." Can this
eminent Victorian really be a guide?
He urges me to study the elder Gods of Time,
the cults of lesser gods obscured or erased:
Kronos, bound to his dreaming sleep
on the farthest island; Kala, less showy
and less tractable than his wild wife Kali;
the unbribable Ifa; Zurvan, the source
of the dualities that create and ever threaten
to destroy the human world, and their ending.
"You'll find clues in my books," Bulwer-Lytton
suggests modestly. I remember dimly
that the author of the world's worst opening line

had other acts. In a novel secret orders take for truth
he disinterred Zanoni, a Chaldean Time Lord
who steps into immortality and comes out again,
because (why else?) he falls in love with a woman.

—*September 18, 2009*

PROTEUS

I am in many forms before I am bound.
I am the starwalker who won't come down.
I am the pond dweller who won't come up.
I am a hawk on a hill.
I am a bear in a berry wood.

I am the giant of the deep
who walked the earth for ten thousand years
before he went back to the sea.
I am the sleeping king
who mated with the earth
and dropped his horns in due season
and grew them back.

I am the blasted oak that drew the lightning.
I am the Man in the Moon.
I am the Hanged Man, and the Emperor, and the Fool.
I am medicine and I am poison.
I am the springing tiger and the quaking goat.
I am the one who makes a prison of the world.
I am the one who makes the world his playground.
I am the death lord on his dark throne.
I am a hummingbird courting a flower.

I am the heaven bird in the World Tree
and the dragon coiled at its roots
and the squirrel that makes mischief between them.
I am a shard from a mirror
that was broken in transit from a blue star.

To release me, you must tie me down.

—December 6, 2009

Becoming Caduceus

I

Kraken Rider

–

The drowned moon of the monster's eye fills my sight
but I cannot lose track of the cruel beak below.
What you most fear is what you must do.
I twist to avoid its flailing tubes and hooks
and stabbing beak, and grapple with slimy pulp
until I can swing up onto its back
and scissor my legs behind its bulbous head.
It thrashes and spins, and I struggle to hold on.
Then it plunges deep, and I see my life passing
until I find I have gills and the scaled body
that can go as deep as the kraken takes me.
I will bend it to a purpose. I will ride the sea-beast
to fight the sea's enemies, those who foul the waters
and poison the fish with the toxic waste of their greed.

–

My sea-father gallops across the whitecaps.
Laughing, he asks if I've had enough knightly adventure
for now. He wants me to follow the sea spray
to the land, to a snow-capped mountain
that belongs to him. I ride the kraken
to the shore, where I am stripped of deepwater things

and emerge naked and golden to receive a new mount.
The winged horse carries me to Helicon,
to the unyielding block that must be opened by force
to release Hippocrene water of inspiration.

-II
HOOVES ON HELICON

–

Harder. The hooves drive sparks from the rock.
The great wings beat the air, driving a warm wind
across the snowy slopes of the mountain.
Again, the hooves come down. And again.
The rock groans and yields, releasing the jets
of the secret spring. I am down on my knees,
catching the water in my open mouth.
Shockingly cold and pure, it floods my senses
and a figure takes form before me, from the mist.
I know her as grey-eyed Clio, muse of History.
Her sister appears at my other side. I know she is
Sophrosyne, or Tempering. She is not on the roll call
of muses; she has come because I need her instruction.
Above my feminine guides, huge as the mountain,
is their mother, Memory. Knowing is remembering.
I am here to help people remember the origin
and purpose of their lives. My sun-father shines
a blessing on the peak, twin ravens, black and white.

III

LIVING AS CADUCEUS

Now the winged horse takes me to the temple mount
where the snake woman waits for me, gripping
her twin serpents by their necks, holding them out
like six-shooters. With proud breasts and flashing eyes
she dares me to receive the power. I open my body
to her cold companions. They slip softly inside me,
interweaving and rising. Now their coils are around me.
Their heads meet at my third eye and I see that
I am become a living caduceus. Powered by the goddess,
I will now do the work of the god who mediates
between humans and deities. He reveals himself
in the play of natural things, through pure synchronicity.

-

Now I have ridden the kraken, and drunk from
the Hippocrene spring, and conformed my body,
inside and out, to the code of the double spiral,
I will speak and act from the best the Greeks know:
Gnothi seauton. Know yourself.
Sophrosyne. Tempering.
Ethos anthropoi daimon. Character is fate.
Anamnesis. Knowing is remembering.
The soul has the ability to conform to its character
the destiny that is allotted to it.

—February 26, 2010

77

White Shadows

When you walk, usually you don't see
the white shadow walking beside you
who may stray behind a hedgerow
or veer away into a dark wood
or a tall city full of thrusting agendas
different from your own, or into a love bower
you left behind, or never made.

Your co-walker may swap places
with another white shadow, and another.
This is a parallel self who made other choices,
who stayed with your former lover,
or still works in the old job, or never crossed the sea,
or chose pancakes instead of waffles for breakfast.
Though the veil between you is thinner
than shrink-wrap, you rarely see through it
except in your dreams, where you enter the life
of an alternate self who has trouble remembering
the alternate self you inhabit this side of the dreamlands.

Yet when your paths converge with a parallel self,
you feel something, obscurely, a tilt to the day,
and may notice you are drawing events and encounters

in a different way. People praise you or put you down
in ways you can't fathom unless you awaken to how
you are loaded now with karma of your white shadow
incurred in adventures you can't know about
until you follow the dream tracks of your multitudinous self.

—September 17, 2010

NIGHT CALLS

The wind came over last night
and hugged me so hard,
my cabin lifted off its foundations
and whirled me west, over moonlit waves,
to the Dream Kin who call me out of time
into the All-at-Once. Eucalyptus people
took off their clothes and danced with delight.

Nature is very personal here.
Wind and wave, moon and stars,
the feigned death of a monarch butterfly
lying still as a fallen leaf, waiting for the sun
to warm it back to drink milkweed,
and the owl who called me three times
and then, not content with my quality of attention,
thirty times more, around midnight
when the glow at my skylight was exactly the blue
of the launch chamber of an Egyptian star traveler.

So many night calls that when I go for my mail,
I remember a box I had long forgotten.
Not the letter drop at my door, or a metal drawer
at the post office, but an old-time box on a post

at the edge of the Street of Dreams.

How could I have forgotten this?

I open it, and find it stuffed with unread night mail
including letters and cards and legal documents
and business papers from a woman I loved and lost
who left the world of pain, shockingly, before me.

I know I will need to travel to her return address
from the place where fresh water joins the salt
when the moon lays a path across the waves.

—February 11, 2011

KIN TO LIGHTNING

Drummer in the clouds,
you awaken me.

In childhood, you put a spear
of bright fire through my body.
I did not die.
I did not even cry out.

When I was in the dark water,
you leaned over me
and told me to get out.

When you came to my farm
and moved over the barn roof
as a serpent of red fire,
you were kindly,
choosing to ground yourself
in the one unlikely place
that left us safe, but awake.

On a night among strange days
you fired your bolts into the corn
like a long-range gunner
homing in on a target

until you accepted the embrace
of the white oak that knew you well.

Soul of Thunder, Bright Awakener,
may I ride with you
on your return journeys
to your kingdom above the clouds.

—April 5, 2011

GRAIL NIGHT

Knight, you came to this crossing before,
bold and green, fired up for the quest,
and did not know that this was always the place:
this stony beach, the crabbers and fishing nets,
the wind-blown houses across the dark waters.
Now you have ridden your horse to the ground;
your armor is rusted, your sword crusted with blood,
your hair bleached to bone. You can see now
that no adversary bested you except yourself;
you refused no battle, fled from no fight.
But in your war for the world you forgot
the world-behind-the-world you were fighting for.
You don't like what you see in the mirror of the water.

Plate by plate, iron by iron, chain by chain,
you cast off your armor. This is taking off your skin.
You are so raw, a teasing zephyr tears your flesh.
You cling to your sword, but the waves rebuff you.
To make this crossing, you must lay down your arms.
In unsteady hands, you raise the great iron
and bury your pride and your rage in forgiving earth.

Salt eats your flesh. The swell buffets you,
tosses you, hurls you down into stinging sand.

When you come up gasping, black birds batter you
and you know that furies you aroused have found you.
Is it death you have come to meet at this water gate?
You swirl into blackness. When the swirling stops,
you are flat on the far shore, looking up at her lovely face.
"I called you in dreams," she reminds you
with only the edge of reproach. "But year after year
you would not listen. And still, you are here."

In a cathedral room, open to the heavens,
you are washed with light. You remember the quest.
Can the Grail be here? You range through the house
seeking, only to return to the great sky-lit space.
She says, "Be still, and open. Stand like a tree,
open like a flower, like a chalice, at your crown."
You remember the crown you once wore
and you let that go, and open. "Drink the light."
You drink deep, and something opens deeper in you.
In the cavity of the heart, a cup is filling with light.
Light streams from the heart, pure waterfall, and you know
you have found the Grail, in the one place it can be found.

—*July 15, 2011*

A Place to Write From (Red Ink)

Write from the place that is raw,
from the night when you lost your skin.
Write of the time in the war-torn city
when your heart was a quivering bird in your palm
and the blood pool kept filling, and you knew
no doctor could heal this wound
though the world would end if you failed
to keep the wounded lover alive for three days more.

Write from the night you wished yourself dead
and spirit flew from your heart, winged by your desire,
down to the lightless lands of the dead
that no one escapes without help.
Write from when there was just enough of you topside
to bribe the ferryman with the ribcage boat
and carry home the part of you that married Death.
Remember the promises you made her:
"You'll never be hurt again." "Every day you'll make poetry."

Write from the night you could not keep those promises
and had to hold the young lover in you by force,
rough as a jailer's armlock, soft as lambskin,
when she thought the one you were losing now

was the one she lost before. And when your heart
breaks again, hold her fast, willing a greater power
to embrace and join you, and write from that.
Dip your pen in the blood pool. This is the time for red ink.

—*July 31, 2011*

SANCTUARY

There are traffic lights in the trees.
Green to red is too sudden for me;
I wait for the blue light to go.
Fallen leaves are yellow spark plugs.
The sun rises in a cape of rainbow feathers.
There is green fire in the eyes of all women.

All roads begin and end here
where the woods meet the water.
I shuffle memories of the future
and prepare for the past that lies ahead.

Here, now: all that I was or will be.
I am the red priest who makes love
to the insatiable Fire Lady.
I am the killer whale with the spirit fin
who swallows souls to keep them safe.
I am the Bear of battles,
a dreamer made to save a lost kingdom,
and I am the sleeping king
who must be awakened again and again.

I am the boy who knows the ways of dragons.
I am the tiger that guards the flock.

I am the stump of the old tree
that is putting up fresh shoots.
I am the stag of the mountain
who drops his antlers and grows them again.
I am one who grows back.

Here and now, I know this:
I love to swim in the bright dark pools
of your eyes, where a child of wonder
darts from under the lilies to welcome me.

Leave it to the fisher boy with the boat
to fetch and carry messages to the world;
leave it to the faithful knight with the long sword
to guard this sanctuary. In another moment of Now
I will unfold again the long leather wallet
that holds the game of the world.

I sense the ripple from a great wave
not yet seen, from Atlantis not yet fallen.
Yet here and now, as you pluck the strings,
and lives and times are dragonflies on the wing,
I drink the wind, I smell the rain,
I breathe in color, I dream a world
of love and peace. Here and now.

—*March 8, 2012*

WILD CHERRIES

The cherry trees are disconsolate lovers;
they can't hold their pink smiles
after the unkindness of that night.
The wind here is straight from Chicago—
it will snap you unless you bend.
The news from far-off money towns
is the clamor of falling towers.

Yet my woolly dog is happy chasing
a well-chewed stick and a wet spaniel,
a green-headed duck is talking quarks
with a brown-headed duck on the lake shore,
and my friend is reading poems of spring
in a language she knows only in dreams.
The wild cherries will bloom again.

—April 9, 2012

ANONWARA (TURTLE DREAMING)

I am the turtle that does not hide.
I wear the armor of a knight, not a skulker.
My vulnerable belly says, Get me if you can;
I stick my neck out.

You call me slow, but on water
I am faster than you, and fast on land.
Deep down, I am the teacher you need
to show you how to fight the Dark One.

I am the broad back you live on.
Ignore me for too long,
go on harming my other children,
and I will shake you off my back.

—*April 16, 2012*

BECAUSE

She says, "I am here because
I got stuck in a garden hose."
He says, "I am here to free my ancestors
from the stories that bind them."
She says, "I am here to find my home star."
He says, "I am here because you showed me paradise
and then told me I could not stay with you forever."
I am here because peregrine falcons
love to live on the edge in the spray of the falls.

There are dreams you should not follow;
there are pictures you should let slip from your wall.
There are memories of the future you can change.
There is one dream you must follow
so you can say to your Death, next time he calls,
"I did not leave that undone.
I did not let my courage fail me.
I did not obstruct water when it should flow."

Time rushes toward you from the future
through the teeth of a savage god.
Don't freeze in the pie-shaped office,

don't leave your body in the pizza oven.

Jump down the hole to the secret of life

before the lion comes. Find an answering flame,

play with the young girls on the pier,

keep the lively dead on speed dial,

carry Midwest mermaids to water.

Mail love apples, juggle the twelve lights,

smell the burning when rain falls through red cedars.

—April 22, 2012

WOMEN DREAM DREAMS THAT WOULD TERRIFY MEN

The mouse dreams dreams that would terrify the cat.

Women dream dreams that would terrify men.

She comes home from the spa, fragrant with honey and
     cucumber,

and tells him, "I could lick myself right now."

In a different mood, she takes a wicked chef's knife

and hacks a stick of pepperoni into limp slices.

In satin tights, fighting for her rights,

she picks likely lovers by their smell

and rides them at a gallop until they are dead.

Jesus Christ is her red-hot lover,

and he fixes her French toast in the morning;

but she is not confined to his church.

Some nights she calls up George Clooney

or a young George Harrison, while Brad Pitt paints her toenails.

She allows her lovers one orgasm for a hundred of hers.

She hangs the occasional boyfriend from the ceiling in chains,

slathered in creamy oatmeal, and consumes all of him when
     hungry.

OR

She sets fierce conditions for her love.

No man may have her unless he serves the Goddess in her.

No suitor may kiss her lips unless he brings her

a bouquet of poems, freshly picked.

No man may know her until he descends to the dark places

where she has been and helps to rescue her lost girls

and makes a place where life is safe and fun for them.

Her mate must twine with her as honeysuckle

and romp with her as a tiger at play

and make love to her in mid-air, beating wings.

He must stir the vast ocean of her womanhood

until wave upon wave breaks over her innermost islands.

She is Goddess and she knows it.

Women dream dreams that would terrify men.

—July 27, 2012

EMPATHY DREAMS

When you weep for all you have lost
I listen with my mouth open;
your tears fall on my tongue
and I taste your pain.

When you were in the river of tiny fish
I splashed with you.
When you hug your swelling belly
I breathe love songs in your ear
to welcome the spirit who is coming
into this world through you.

When they broke the child in you
something broke in me.
When you fled from the johns to the jones
I tried to crack your crystal palace
so you could visit that beautiful boy
who found refuge with Peter Pan.

I was with you when they beat you
for sucking your thumb, and when they
beat you harder because you couldn't kill
the lovely soft bandit cornered by coon dogs.

I am with you at the white table
of the one who has shared his cup with you.

I laugh with you when you cartwheel through life
as a circus acrobat, and when you
walk the high wire without fear
because your second self goes ahead of you
making footholds so you cannot fall.

At the border camp. I share your terror
of returning to a country you can't remember
where killers still haunt the killing fields.
I am with the scary man with brick dust
on his skin and a claw hammer in his belt.
I whisper to him, "Don't tread on wildflowers."

I am with then hunter and the hunted.
I am Cossack and Jew, slave and slave owner.
I am the man in iron from the dragon boat.
I am the priestess whose weapons
are a mirror and the sickle moon,
who can give blood to the earth without cutting.

I am in the blade of grass that bends
under the tremendous gray hoof, and springs back.
I am with the elephant mother who grieves

for her calf as metal rain from the poachers' gunship
turns her dreams to blood ivory.

I am no bodhisattva, able to remember
all lives, past and present, without being overwhelmed.
I must spit out the tears I have tasted
and not go stooped under grief and pain of others.

But I can do this: I can go to the one
with a hole in the heart, and show you
the precious child who fled from your body
when they tried to kill your dreams,
and you lost the dreamer in you.

I can promise your child of wonder
that, despite everything, you are safe and can be fun.
I can hold you together until you know each other.
Growing beyond myself, I can go on holding you
in the fierce embrace of Great Mother Bear
until you cannot be apart, because you are one.

—September 14, 2012

PART II

TALES FROM THE IMAGINAL REALM

AT THE GATE OF STORY

THE GATEKEEPERS cannot see where the tide of pilgrims begins. Its source lies far to the north, beyond the Pillars of Hercules, the olive groves and forests of cork, even beyond the stern keep of the man of iron dreams on a high wind-raked plateau. The travelers are so many that their feet have emptied the strait, making a land bridge between the continents. Such was the report of one who reached the Gate of Story.

Yawning on their cushioned seats by a wall bleached to the color of smilodon bones, the gatekeepers do not rule on the veracity of this account. Like the knight of La Mancha, they know that facts can be the enemy of truth. Judging the truth of a story by whether it stirs or disturbs the hearer, they turn away the man who parted the seas. Too many others have tried to pawn this story before; it has been drained of surprise.

"Altagracia!" croaks a man whose flesh has fallen away so his linen suit hangs off him like a flag of defeat. Some in the crowd cross themselves or finger amulets against the evil eye. An imam directs a boy to offer the parched traveler a waterskin. "Altagracia!" the man cries again, water frothing from his cracked lips.

—No one has spoken that name at this gate before. The gatekeepers motion for the man who has used it to be advanced to the front of the line. Camel drivers open a way for him with their switches, without regard for the age or gender of those they are beating back.

—"You have three minutes," says the chief keeper of the Gate of Story. He flourishes a pocket watch and spins it, on its chain, from his long pointing finger.

—"She is Altagracia," the story man begins. . . .

She is very pale, with lustrous black hair and black eyes. Her travel-ing clothes are the color of sand in shadow. She wears a veil under her hat. She has pushed it back, but it can be drawn over her face to keep off blowing sand and flies. She has a good deal of luggage, including a hatbox, handled with ease by her giant black servant, Fidel, who has been assigned by her father, The Professor, to keep her safe. Fidel can speak only in little mewling sounds, which the cats of the city understand. His tongue was cut out, perhaps at his own volition, to guarantee that he will live up to his name, which means "faithful," when it comes to keeping secrets, since he is also illiterate.

Each time the story of Altagracia is told, it expands, and the world with it. Last time I spoke of her, she did not have dogs, but now she has a pair of them, resembling greyhounds, that she calls her sight hounds. I said that Fidel is illiterate and mute, but as I speak his shadow is slipping ahead of him through the city gate in the form of a black cat. It is running into the Sultan's library, where it stands on its hind legs to remove a precious copy of the seventh volume of Pliny Maior's Natural History *from a cabinet that others always find locked. The feline Fidel, unlike his human counterpart, can speak. He will go to the harem and delight his hearers all night long with the exact descriptions of dog-headed men, Triballes who kill with a look, and lions with the tails of scorpions. He will be rewarded with dishes of sherbet and leg-humping until the chief eunuch will order his tongue, or another particle, to be excised. The feline Fidel is not so easily bested. By naming—both in lapidary*

Latin and in the Berberous Arabic of the court—all the creatures of Pliny's hearsay, he has brought them to life. The eunuch's scimitar is no match for a manticore.

It became harder and harder to hear the teller of this tale, because as each word was uttered, the scene and the action around the gate became more profuse. The crowd parted and reformed as animals out of legend galloped and bulled their way through. The shadow of immense wings cooled the hot sand. A ship in full sail appeared on a canal that surely was not there before. A man with his head under a black cloth took pictures on glass of a couple of newlyweds boarding a train whose engine puffed perfect blue smoke rings. A cat that was also smoking, with the aid of an amber cigarette holder, shuffled a Marseilles deck and purred, "Pick a card, any card at all."

The head gatekeeper, invoking the Most High, ordered the man who knew Altagracia to pass through the Gate of Story, and threatened to do terrible things to his mother unless he passed through without delay.

"The Gate is closed for today," he announced to the host of story pilgrims. They groaned and wept and raged. Many of them, desperate to be heard, tried to shout their stories over each other, producing a weird cacophony that made the keepers press their hands over their ears. Blue-eyed janissaries appeared on the battlements of the gatehouse and fired warning shots into the air.

In the sudden silence, a voice said in a placeless accent, "You will hear me." The voice belonged to a short, spare man with a clipped goatee, who held an umbrella over his head.

"We will hear no more Namers today," the head keeper spoke in a voice of thunder.

"I am neither a Namer nor an un-Namer. I am the sculptor of the Immortal Sentence."

These words, also, had never been heard at the Gate of Story. The keepers were bound by a rule laid down in the remotest of pasts to give the speaker a hearing.

When I first told this story, it took longer than one thousand and one nights to reach the end. Every day since then, I have shortened the story by a sentence. Now that it fills less than a page, I reduce it by one word in each telling. In this instance reducing is the opposite of reduction. With each word I remove, I approach closer to the quintessence of the tale, which is also the key to the making and unmaking of worlds. The consummation of my art will be to deliver the Immortal Sentence, which will replace the knowledge of the world and become the theme of all branches of a new literature and science. Some have thought that the Immortal Sentence will consist only of four letters. This cannot be known until all the words that veil it have been stripped away.

"Cease speaking!" the head gatekeeper commanded. His composure had been shaken. There was whiteness around his mouth. "You may enter."

The man with the umbrella strode with long decisive steps—unusually fast for a person of small stature, but then he worked his whole legs, from the hips—through the Gate of Story. The immensely high cedar doors began to swing shut. The gatekeepers had gathered their cushions and magic carpets. But the head keeper turned back when a new voice addressed him by his secret name, the name he shared only with Khidr, the guide of those who have no earthly guide.

It was a woman's voice. When he faced her, he was pleased to see that she was veiled, though her features could be seen through the gauzy stuff. Her clothes were of English cut, he thought, made by the finest seamstress. Yet something about her made him think of the forbidden vineyards of Shiraz.

"Come up on the rooftop," she invited him. "We will share a cup of wine."

"Are you a djinn?" he demanded, now fearful.

"I am the Sustainer. Every day, I must repeat the one story that keeps the world turning. Every syllable must be flawless, because this is the code on which the world depends."

"Then why have we never seen you at this gate before?"

"Do you suppose I have only one form?"

"Whatever form you take, if you are repeating a story that has been told before, we will know it, and you will have failed the test."

"You understand very little, and after hearing the story you will know even less. The nature of the story that sustains the world is that it is never different and never the same. By repeating it perfectly, each teller creates a new story and renews the world."

"This defies both God and reason."

"Then listen."

Somehow the head keeper found he was seated beside her on the roof of the watchtower, with the sweet taste of the forbidden wine on his lips.

The veiled woman spoke:

The gatekeepers cannot see where the tide of pilgrims begins. Its source lies far to the north, beyond the Pillars of Hercules, the olive groves and forests of cork, even beyond the stern keep of the man of iron dreams on a high wind-raked plateau. The travelers are so many that their feet have emptied the strait, making a land bridge between the continents. Such was the report of one who reached the Gate of Story.

MOON TIGER

THE FACE OF THE MOON is turning red as earth's shadow falls across it. As the moon darkens, the red war-star, Antares, burns brighter. The moon is caught in the pincers of the Scorpion, and its light is going out.

The kids who were necking in an old Chevy pickup on the far side of the parking lot have stopped to watch. They think it's cool to be out under a lunar eclipse. I don't think it's so cool. Strange howls, neither animal nor human, carry far across the night. They could be the cries of predators, or victims. Pleasure or pain. It's all mixed up. It's all edgy.

I don't want to be here, but I was called. There will be many visitors from Luna tonight, but not the bright spirits. When the bright face of the moon is darkened, the beings of the dark side have a window of opportunity. It comes only once or twice a year, sometimes only once in several years.

The gatekeepers can't stop all of them from coming through, though some fight and die in the attempt.

There are not many of us left in the cities who can see, even obscurely, what is taking place. Most of us have lost our night vision, and military goggles are no substitute for what I am talking about. The few who can see in the dark, but lean toward the light, must work now to defend earth from the forces of chaos and war that are riding toward us from the moon in a wild hunt.

I am here, in the parking lot of a supermarket on Long Island, because I know the beast that is coming. It is my duty to meet it, and wrestle with it, and hold and gentle its wild energy if I can. If I fail, I will be one of those brought down by a stun gun or knockout darts—or by live police bullets—before morning, to snarl at other lunatics from a cage or to claw at the walls of a padded cell. This is the night when the lunar spirits among us can most easily become lunatics.

"Aw baby," the boy in the car groans into his girlfriend's ear. "Do you feel that, like the power?"

Her response is a scream, which soon recedes into an unpleasant gurgling and gagging. I don't need to look to know that blood is gushing from her neck, not in a dreamy, erotic flow like that induced in vampire movies, but in a torrent from the arteries of her neck. The boy—or rather, what is working through him—has struck as deep as human teeth can go.

I see this in a flash, but the flash is a memory of the near future, something that has not yet taken root in this world.

I bound toward the pickup, growling low in my throat.

I grab for the passenger door, drag it open, and pull the girl out. Her clothes are in disarray. Her bra has been unhooked, and her breasts bounce as I drag her from the high cab of the pickup.

"What the fuck?" Her boyfriend hurls himself after us. His unzipped jeans drop to his ankles, and he trips and falls on his face.

"Come to me." I am not speaking to him, or his girlfriend. I am speaking to the thing that is with him, but not yet in him. In the sodden dark of the moon, I can see its immense form, moving around the boy. But it has not yet revealed its face.

"Leave the kid," I tell the thing from the dark moon. "He is nothing. A poor toy. He is not worthy of you. He is not one of our kind."

I feel the beast's recognition. In his lust and impatience, he plunges around the kid, spinning the gangling body.

"You know me," I encourage him. "We are brothers. Join me and we will eat together."

The boy is spinning like a top, puking and yelping.

The beast shows his face. It projects from the back of the boy's head, the jaws open to reveal the murderous curve of the canines. He is beautiful, and he is death. His stripes fall across an immense field of white fur, bright and elegant as the full moon before its darkening. His eyes are blood red.

The girl is screaming. I don't know whether she can see him, or simply feels his hunger.

The moon tiger drops the boy like a rag doll.

He leaps at me, and I receive him. When he enters my energy field, I feel myself expand to many times my normal size. When he comes inside my solar plexus, I am seized by his rage and hunger. He wants me to tear and rend, to spring on the girl, to rip out her lover's throat and liver. I fight with him, deep within my own being. I leave the parking lot and go down into the cavernous space he has entered. I track him through a dark forest toward a clearing where everything smells like delicious food, food I must have. The food looks like baby lambs and chickens. What is the harm in killing them? It's no worse than eating chicken or meat that comes shrink-wrapped from the supermarket, and maybe it's morally superior, since I am doing the butchering myself. I lope after a lamb, enjoying my speed and strength. I am on top of my meal when I realize that the lamb is the girl in the parking lot.

I veer away in time to avoid savaging her. I shake myself violently, trying to shake off the force of his will that is riding me. I see him again as a separate being, a beautiful killing machine. We fight, tooth and claw, evenly matched, until both of us are raw and dripping with blood.

I tell him, with the bravura of a condemned man, "You can't win. You are inside me."

He hesitates for a moment, just long enough for me to lay open his chest. I rip his steaming heart from the chest cavity and devour it.

"I have you now," he speaks in my mind.

The hunger is ravening. The thirst that now drives me is even worse. I am urgent to lap real blood.

I watch the pickup truck speeding away.

I walk into the market. There are only a few people in the store at this hour, talking about the eclipse. A Chinese girl says they believed in her family that a lunar eclipse happens when demons eat the moon. She is food. The chubby checkout girl is also food. The moon tiger wants them.

I feel his resistance as I go down the aisles. It wavers just a little as I approach the butcher's counter, and revives in full force when we see that the butcher shop is closed for the night.

I go along the aisle to the meat coolers and select half a dozen shrink-wrapped steaks, the ones that look reddest and bloodiest, and a four-pound economy package of chopped meat.

In my saliva glands, in my gut and sinews, the moon tiger protests that he wants different food.

Be a good boy, I tell him, or I'll go back to being a vegetarian.

"That was wild," Maddy, the chubby girl at the check-out tells me, referring to the eclipse. "I'm kinda glad it's over. People were freakier than ever tonight."

I grunt, noncommittal, hoping that I was not one of the people who looked freaky.

Maddy scans all my packages of meat. "You must be hav-
ing some barbecue. Weren't you a vegetarian?"

"I got over it."

THE XIBALBA EXCHANGE

"I CAN'T GET AWAY from a dream," Emily Lejeune explained her reason for coming to see me. As she said this, the light went out in her eyes, and her shoulders slumped forward. The lively, birdlike woman I had greeted at the door suddenly looked fifteen years older.

"Then you had better tell me."

"This dream is very old. I had it fifteen years ago."

"There's no such thing as an old dream. When we go dreaming, we step outside time. Why not go ahead and tell me the dream, just as you remember it."

She half-closed her eyes. "I am in several places at once—on board a plane and watching the whole scene at the same time. The plane explodes in midair. The carnage is terrible. I see it close up. I see people decapitated, limbs torn away. I see the body pieces among the wreckage. Carnage, carnage, carnage."

She was sobbing now. Her body seemed to cave inward. I placed my hands gently on her shoulders, sheltering. Then I passed her the box of Kleenex I always keep handy for clients.

"You say you had this dream fifteen years ago."

"Yes."

"And it felt like a literal plane crash?"

"Oh yes, it was entirely real. I can still see the body parts."

"There have been a lot of tragedies involving plane crashes since then. And of course the 9/11 horror. Is it possible you dreamed an event that has manifested since the dream?"

"Yes, absolutely."

"Then we need to understand the link. Do you know anybody who has died in a plane crash?"

"No." She was quite definite.

"Is it possible that somebody close to you lost a loved one in a plane crash?"

"I don't think so."

"There must be some connection. Of course, we are all connected. Mass tragedies seem to throw a shadow before them. Perhaps you are experiencing the burden of the prophetic dreamer, who foresees terrible events but can find no way to prevent them."

She stared at me. "Is that why I have lost my dreams? I feel that plane crash put a lid on my dreaming. I haven't remembered a dream in all the years since it happened."

"Then perhaps we can help you to dream wide awake, here in this room. Are you willing to try that?"

Emily nodded.

I guided her through a simple meditation I have used with many people, to put them in touch with more of their own gifts and possibilities than they may recognize, and to bring through lost energy.

"I want you to sit in a comfortable upright position and follow the flow of your breathing. That's right. You may want to close your eyes. Now I want you to let me guide you with my voice on a journey through your own energy anatomy. We are going to travel through the seven major chakras, or energy centers. Are you willing to do that?"

She nodded again.

"You are going down to the root center. In terms of your body, this is located at the base of your spine and encompasses the whole area down to the soles of your feet. The root center involves your connection to the Earth, to your ancestry, to the means of physical life and survival. You are journeying down to the mouth of a cavern. It's dark and blurry to begin with, but now you are beginning to discern a color. You are entering into the cavernous space of the root center, and you are becoming aware there is something that lives here. Can you sense it?"

"Yes."

"Can you make out its shape?"

"Yes. It is coiled. It may be a dragon."

"How do you feel?"

"I'm okay with it. It's sleeping right now."

"Let's go up a level. Now you are approaching the entrance to the second chakra, your sex-creative center. We're going inside. We need to see what flows, or is blocked in this center, and what lives here."

"No!"

"What is it?"

"It's something huge. It has multiple legs or tentacles. Something like a spider, or an octopus."

"How do you feel?"

"I'm scared."

"Where do you see it?"

"It's not in me so much as on me."

"What do you need to do?"

"I need to get it off."

"All right, let's see how we can deal with it."

She excused herself to go to the bathroom. I had the curious idea, while waiting for her, that the spiderish thing and the plane crash dream were related.

"I'm sorry," she said when she came back. "I can't go any further right now."

I was disappointed, but not willing to push. "I can see you at the same time tomorrow. Will you come back?"

"Yes."

"Then will you accept a couple of homeplay assignments? First, I want you to approach the night with intention. Ask for guidance on what brought you here. Don't worry if you don't remember a dream when you wake up. Just write down whatever is with you—first thoughts, feelings, sensations. Our dreams give us guidance even when we don't remember the dreams.

"Second, I'd like you to play the game of accepting any unusual or striking thing that enters your field of perception between now and our appointment tomorrow as a message from the world. The first thing that is playing on the car radio, the bumper sticker on the car ahead of you, a snatch of conversation from a stranger at the supermarket checkout, really anything at all. Will you do that?"

Emily readily agreed.

I very much hoped she would come back. In many of my cases, whenever a major healing or life-change is within range, the client reaches a point of resistance where they must choose between a breakthrough and a breakdown.

Naturally, I consulted my own dreams for insight on Emily's case. I dreamed again of the Anubis, the Egyptian Gate-keeper. He met me in the woods and we went swimming together. The dream did not relate directly to Emily's situation, but I rose from it with an immense sense of well-being and the joyous sensation of the intimate presence of a larger power, filling out my energy field.

I honored my dream by foregoing my morning coffee and journaling and going directly down to the lake.

A pair of young boys, possibly six years old, were playing in a sandpit on the lake beach. As I passed, one said to the other, "The Sacred Beasts aren't the very best. The Egyptian gods are."

I stood stock-still for a moment, hardly daring to believe what I had just heard. I presume that the boys were discussing video games, or comic book characters. But their words evoked the heart of my own calling. I did not yet know that this message from the world was exact counsel on what was about to unfold.

I quickly swam to the ropes, and under them, through the lakeweed, out into open water beyond the legal enclosure. The warm summer sun, playing over cool currents, gave me the sense of swimming across a vast liquid zebra skin, from a warm stripe through a cool stripe, on and on past the floating docks to the far headland. With every minute in the green and amber lake, I felt stronger. As I swam back, I felt myself plowing the waters, pushing myself forward at ever greater speed.

Some of the people inside the ropes glowered at me disapprovingly. Couldn't I read the sign? As I waded back through the legal enclosure to the shore, I noticed a very dead fish floating dead in the water, among the people inside the ropes. The fish were very much alive outside the rules. A second message for the day, perhaps for any day

Emily was only five minutes late, bumping up the drive in her little hatchback.

"I remembered a dream," she told me. "But it was the same dream. Wreckage and carnage, all over again."

"Anything else?"

"I went to this bookstore where they have good coffee. And I saw this notecard."

She placed it on my desk. It showed an enormous spider descending a wall towards two people lying in the same bed.

The spider was bigger than the sleeping humans. I turned the card over. "Spider am Morgen" was the title on the back.

"Okay, so what's the message?" I challenged Emily.

"It's time to clear this stuff."

"Excellent. Will you tell me the dream of the plane crash again?"

When she had finished I told her, "I have the strong feeling that you experienced a psychic tug from someone who was on the plane. Are you absolutely certain you don't know anyone who died in a plane crash?"

"I already told you. No, I don't know anyone who died like that."

I followed my gut instinct to stay on this. As we talked, I could see some elements of the airplane cabin quite distinctly—the bright colors of the flight attendant's uniforms, the swirl of terror and confusion as the plane went down.

"Will you think again? Maybe the connection is through a friend who knew someone on the plane. Is it possible you are connected—through a mutual acquaintance—with someone you never met who died in a plane crash?"

"O my God!" Emily gasped. "I do know someone who died in a plane crash. I never met her, but she was flying from Guatemala to meet me."

"From Guatemala?"

"Yes, she was coming to do some spiritual work with me. The plane she was on crashed about three years after my dream."

"What is her name?"

"I never knew her name."

"Then how did you make the connection with her?"

"It was through a spiritual network. I can't talk about it. I have never told anyone about this." She was too scared to say more, and I did not push for further details.

Mystery upon mystery.

I started scanning. Very rapidly, I found myself inside a world of Central American witches and curanderos. I saw a huge black jaguar prowling, and remembered a Mayan shaman who had once visited me in his energy form, a web of greenish light in the shape of a jaguar.

"What do you know about Mayan shamans?"

"Not a lot. But I have been to several Mayan sites and I felt a strong affinity. On one of the stepped pyramids, I felt I had stepped into a past life."

I was trying to grasp what had happened with the Guatemalan woman on the plane. She worked with the Mayan traditions, with some overlay, something borrowed from voodoo or European witchcraft. As the plane went down, in her terror, Maya reached for the woman who was waiting for her in Toronto. As she flew towards Emily, in her second body, a part of Emily left her own body and traveled to the exploding plane. Somehow, this part of Emily had been sucked down into a Mayan underworld, a Land of the Dead for which she was not intended.

I was quite certain that this was at the root of Emily's terror and her sense that she was missing a vital part of herself.

At the moment of death, a soul exchange had taken place.

Part of Maya's soul, fleeing the plane crash, had latched onto Emily. I saw it quite clearly, attached to the liver by crab-like pincers, holding on tight. Emily perceived this in her own way when she described the spider-thing at her second chakra.

In the horror and carnage of the plane wreck, a part of Emily, passing through Maya, was sucked into an after-death experience that was meant for Maya. This part of Emily was sucked all the way down into Xibalba, a death world of the Mayan imagination that is a real shithole. In Mayan reliefs, the death lords of Xibalba are shown farting immense poisonous clouds. Down in Xibalba, everything smells like shit, and turns to shit. Not a habitat anyone in their right mind would choose to visit for any purpose. Furthermore, in the Mayan tales the lords of Xibalba are extremely disinclined to allow any visitor to leave.

Part of Emily was in this hell because of a soul swap that had taken place without her consent. It was not clear to me whether "Maya" had deliberately brought about this exchange, or whether it happened spontaneously, in the terror and confusion of the plane wreck.

The only chance of bringing Emily's soul part up from the underworld was to try to negotiate an exchange with the lords of Xibalba. This would require us to give them the soul that belonged to them—the one that had been attached for more than a decade to Emily's liver.

"I am going to journey for you," I announced to Emily. "With your permission, I will travel where I need to go in order to clear this business. We'll darken the room—because it is easier to see with inner light when external light is excluded—and I'll put on a drumming tape, which provides energy and focus."

"What do you want me to do?"

"I want you to stay comfortably seated, very much in your body, and focused on your intention. What is your intention?"

"I want clearing."

"Perfect. So you will not journey. You will stay focused on your intention, and you will open your heart to a gift that may come to you, a gift of something that belongs to you. I would like to hold your hand during the journey. Would that be all right with you?"

"Of course."

I spoke words that invoke the Gatekeeper. "Opener of the Ways, guide me safely through the Otherworld."

I felt the intimate and immensely powerful presence of Anubis. It would be insane—quite possibly suicidal—to enter

Xibalba without heavy-duty support. But I felt strong, surrounded by Egyptian powers that were entirely familiar with the realms of death. And I felt the supportive presence of the black jaguar, a guide who knew the territory. I was not sure how Egyptian deities would get on with Mayans, but I was willing to work with what was with me.

I covered my eyes and let the heartbeat of the drumming carry me. The path for my journey was clear. I would descend to Xibalba, confront its death lords, and seek to negotiate the exchange. If this could be accomplished on the imaginal plane, it would need to be concluded and sealed by certain physical actions. I had a notion of what these might be; I would speak to Emily about these things after my journey.

I felt the energy form of Anubis strengthening within and around my own. My shoulders broadened and my chest grew deeper. I saw with his eyes, smelled with his keen senses. We plunged down and down into the Mayan shithole. It smelled awful. As we made our landing, I stood within a blazing circle of light.

The death lords of the Mayan underworld and their creatures—some resembling monstrous flies that live on dung—sniffed and rumbled around my landing area. I threw my trading-thing before them, the part of Maya's soul that had stayed with Emily. It had been captured in a doll constructed from a piece of wood and colorful fabric, but it looked like—and was—a miniature Maya. The death lords wanted fresh blood as well, so I conjured a blood offering.

A frightened young woman was allowed to emerge from the shadows. She also appeared as a miniature figure, part woman and part bird, with the bright feathers of the quetzal. Under Egyptian guard, I flew up from the Mayan hell, sealing the gate behind me.

As I approached Emily, I held the bird-soul in my cupped hands. I opened my hands and blew. The bird-woman divided into two. The part that was a younger Emily flew into her open heart. And a tiny quetzal bird flew on bright wings into her third eye.

I discussed with Emily what I had experienced—a real event on the imaginal plane that would now require physical action to complete the transaction and fulfill the conditions of the death lords of Xibalba. She readily agreed to make a doll, starting with a flat piece of wood she would dress with colorful fabrics. The blood requirement was one we hoped could be fulfilled with a fresh piece of raw liver. Emily said she would get this from the village. We agreed to meet at that evening to conduct the ritual.

When Emily returned at the agreed time, I was disappointed to learn that she had not been able to acquire raw liver.

"But I got premium sirloin steak, New York strip."

I was not convinced that this would be enough to satisfy the thirsty lords of Xibalba, but we would make the trial.

We walked a little-used path into the woods and found a place where the earth, under the leaves, was soft and moist and loamy. I helped Emily to dig a hole on a downward slope with a little hand trowel. I asked the powers to help us release what belonged in the earth, and what belonged in the higher realms. With my help, Emily held the bloody meat against her liver, with the doll behind it.

When the doll was interred and covered, we all felt a clearing, an influx of light.

The night brought peaceful dreams to both of us.

I still wondered whether a piece of steak from a supermarket was enough to fulfill the blood obligation.

In the morning, Emily arrived without an appointment as I was sipping my coffee on the porch. She was bursting to tell me what she had accomplished overnight.

"I knew that the blood had to come from me. But I can't make my period come on demand. However, it came early last night. I was able to return to the burial place and I gave my blood to the earth."

This seemed quite perfect. In the Mayan reliefs, royals are shown offering blood drawn from their own bodies. Kings pierced their tongues and their penises. For woman, however, it is not necessary to cut—let alone kill—to offer blood sacrifice.

A STRANGER CAME to our town. He spoke with a foreign accent, and his ways were different. Some people said he came from Amsterdam, others said he was from Venice. Soon the rumor spread that he was a magician. People began to visit him, usually in the hours of darkness, because this was a very respectable town and none of the burghers or their wives wished to be seen consorting with a magician.

One night the wife of a wealthy merchant mounted the steps to his brownstone and raised her hand, trembling a little, to the lion's head knocker on the door. She raised the knocker, but did not let it fall because she was suddenly so nervous and embarrassed, she felt ready to flee back to her own comfortable home. But the door opened smoothly and noiselessly, and she found herself flowing down a long hall and through the open door of a study where a fire crackled in the grate.

The magician received her in a dressing gown of oriental design, embroidered with dragons and tigers, and did not apologize for smoking a cigar.

He addressed her by name—Eva—directed her to a comfortable easy chair, and proceeded to describe to her the most intimate details of her life. "Your life is airless," he told her. "You cannot breathe in it."

This so exactly evoked her own feelings that she was ready to appoint him her guru, shrink, and personal trainer. "Tell me what I must do. I will do whatever you say." The magician shook his head.

"You must take responsibility for your own life."

"Name your fee." She got out her checkbook. "You know we have plenty of money."

The magician shrugged. "You are free to pay me whatever pleases you. But that will not make me the keeper of your soul."

She wept splotchy mascara tears.

"If you wish to know what to do," he told her, "you must listen to your dreams."

But in our town, people had fallen out of the habit of listening to dreams, to the point where many questioned whether they dreamed at all. Talk of dreams made the merchant's wife more nervous than before. She explained that she took pills to sleep and woke with an alarm clock into the hurry of her husband's world.

"Very well," the magician told her. "If you cannot listen to your dreams, you must listen to your waking world, which is also a dream and will speak to you in the manner of dreams if you know how to attend to it."

"I don't understand."

"If I were truly a magician, and could give you any help or guidance that you need, what is the one thing—the one thing—you would ask for, from the beating heart of your life?"

"I would ask—oh, I don't know." Her breath came shallow and fast. She felt close to a panic attack. Yet the sense of airlessness was different from at home, and was not to be explained by the haze of cigar smoke. She felt she was trying to breathe at high altitude, from a high mountaintop. "I want to breathe again," the words came at last in a violent exhalation. "How can I breathe again?"

"Very well. You must carry this question with you everywhere during the next week of your life. Write it down." He passed her a small notepad and a pencil. "Carry your question close to your heart." He glanced discreetly at her ample bosom, and she took the hint, folding the note into a tiny square that she hid inside her bra.

"As you go about your life, carrying your question, be alert for anything unusual that happens. Anything striking or unexpected—an accident, a coincidence, a chance encounter—could be a sign from the world. Pay special attention to unexpected encounters. Remember that anything that happens within your field of perception could hold the answer to your question."

Eva agreed to try, though this procedure seemed very strange to her. On the first day, nothing remarkable took place. Her life revolved in its familiar courses, through the rounds of shopping and social engagements.

Toward evening, despondent, Eva sat on a bench in the park in front of the clock tower to watch the sun going down. She noticed a bird on the ground near her left foot. It lay on its side, apparently dead. Her gloom deepened, because she felt she had found the sign from the world she had been told to seek. She told herself, I am like that dead bird. I forgot how to fly, and then the life went out of me.

While she was feeling sorry for herself, a stranger sat down next to her on the bench. When he struck up a conversation, she surprised herself by responding to his questions, looking him boldly in the eye. Under normal circumstances, she would never speak to an unknown man in the park. But this man seemed educated and interesting. His name was Matthew. He spoke of books she had meant to read and places she had meant to go. His hazel eyes were steady and thoughtful, with a twinkle of humor. His fingers were long and slender and beautifully trimmed. After twenty minutes, as she rose to leave, Eva surprised herself again by agreeing to meet him again in the park the next day.

As she started back along the path, Eva glanced down at the bird. She was amazed to see that the seemingly lifeless pigeon was back on its feet. The bird took a few clumsy, waddling steps. Then it beat its wings and took off. Eva watched it sail away over the rooftops.

On her way home, Eva said to herself, "The bird really is my sign. When I got off my butt—when I took a definite action, accepting the risk—then my bird came to life and found its wings."

An image flashed into her mind of herself and the bird as a single being, with her head and the pigeon's body. It looked like something from an Egyptian mummy case. She knew then that the change was accelerating. When she let the world speak to her like a dream, she started seeing dreams inside her head. "I'm wide awake and dreaming," she marveled.

After the dead bird walked, Eva's life was different. Her new friend invited her to a lecture, then a class where she spent a lot of time breathing and stretching but did not feel silly or uncomfortable. Matthew was gentle and loving. He made no overt sexual overtures, which kept things safe but also confused her, since she had no experience of an intimate friendship with a man that did not include sex. She fantasized, more and more vividly, about becoming his lover.

Her husband learned of her friendship and raged at her with jealous accusations. She considered leaving him. But even though the children were grown, she feared going without the money and the comforts she was used to. To appease her husband, she agreed to stop seeing Matthew.

Her life became more wretched than before.

She developed asthma, which had plagued her as a child. She lay awake at night, gasping for breath, or pressing her face deep into a pillow so her husband would not be torn from sleep by her coughing fits.

She drank too much wine at dinner and complained to herself while her husband watched the TV news.

She took more pills to control her moods and shut out her dreams. She considered hoarding enough of her pills to transport herself into dreamless sleep forever.

One day she found herself, without planning it, on the block where the magician lived. She moved, without reflection, up the steps to the door with the lion's head knocker. The magician received her in his study, wearing the same robe. He listened as she described the depth of her unhappiness, the asthma attacks, the thoughts of self-destruction.

The magician said "You got your message from the world. Why did you fail to honor it?"

Squirming a little, she told him that the incident of the resurrected bird, that had seemed so vivid and magical in the park, had dwindled into insignificance in her mind as she was confronted with the hard realities of life—her husband's rage, the worries over money. "It seemed to be only a dream, only a fairytale for children."

The magician rumbled, but summoned his patience and repeated his original counsel. "Shape the question that is at the beating heart of your life and put it to the world. You are responsible for your own reality. In the light of your intention, within the frame of your question, anything the world gives you may be an answering voice."

He did not reveal to her that his instruction echoed the vow he had taken, in another land, when he had been raised up as Magister Ludi of an ancient Order. The oath of his grade, like all important things, was extremely simple. It was an open secret, already known to anyone who was ready to know it. The words of the oath were these:

I will interpret anything that enters my field of perception as a direct message from God to my soul.

The magician asked, "Do you have a new question for the world?"

"I wish to know how I can make my life endurable."

"There is too much 'I' in that question."

"Then I ask to know how I can serve my life's purpose."

"Which life?"

She frowned a little, not understanding.

"Whose life?" he probed. "The little you or the big you? The ego or the soul?"

"I wish to know how I can serve my soul's purpose."

The magician nodded. The question was acceptable. He repeated his instructions on reading the sign language of the world. "Remember, a sign from the world is like a big dream. You are required to act on it. There are doorways in life that are open only at certain times. If you forget your undertaking and come looking for me again, you may find there is no longer a magician at this house. You may find that this house no longer exists."

LOVE TUNNEL

BETH IS THIRTEEN, and it's only a few weeks since her mother found her crying and trying to hide a wad of bloody tissues and gave her certain items "to get you started." Beth is curious about sex and the changes in her body, but horrified at any suggestion of a boyfriend.

Her brothers, Brett and Andy, give her no mercy. She fills in a questionnaire in a magazine about the Ten Worst Things About Being a Teen without drawing breath; she leaves the answer boxes for the Ten Best Things blank.

After school one evening when the moon is full, shining bright on her face, she sits on her bed and makes a wish. "I wish I could just grow up," she tells the moon. "I wish I could grow up without having to be a teen."

She flops down, feeling stupid, and tries to focus on her social studies homework. She is diverted by a gentle whir that might be the dishwasher downstairs, except that the sound is in her room.

In the middle of her room, just above the clothes hamper at the foot of the bed, something is spinning. It is something like a whirlpool made of air. When she looks closer, Beth sees it is actually a tunnel, walled with dense, swirling air. She can see lights and colors at the other end, in a space that is not her room.

Beth considers calling for help. But she's afraid the thing may disappear, and her brothers will ridicule her for "making things up." Also, she wants to keep this discovery to herself, at least until she has figured out what it is.

She leans closer, peering into the tunnel. There is a room on the other side, with pink wallpaper, and there is something thrilling and maybe illicit in that room. The walls of the tunnel are turning and whirling. The thing exerts suction. Beth feels herself being pulled inside.

She jerks away, but a gentle female voice whispers, It's all right, honey. You can come in. The voice is so sweet and familiar, she lets herself go. The suction has her, like a twister, and she is flying through the tunnel. She comes out, very quickly, with an audible pop, in a room she does not recognize.

The room seems unlived-in, like a hotel room. It smells of perfume and body lotion and something like raw fish. There is a suitcase on a folding stand next to the TV cabinet, and a litter of garments on the rug and the end of the bed. There are prints of greyhounds and racehorses on the pink walls.

Someone is rooting around in a little refrigerator, choosing and discarding a series of miniature bottles. It is a man with a large mole on his right shoulder and rank black hair sprouting from his armpits. Beth gasps as he dives deeper into the tiny fridge, because the man is naked all the way down. His butt comes up, mooning her, and she can see something very long and pink swaying below.

Beth is frozen for a long moment before her brain starts ticking, calculating the distance from the bed to the floor, considering the bedside phone. What do you do in a hotel? Call 0 for the operator? Terrified by the naked man, whose thing looks even bigger as he turns, with a leer of triumph on his stubbly chops and a half-bottle of champagne in his fist, Beth hugs herself tight. And finds there is a lot more of her to shield. What's this? Oh jeez, I've got boobs! Fat and round, jutting from her formerly flat chest like honeydew melons.

The man has hair from his collarbones to the black bush at his crotch, where his thing is standing and swaying like a cobra under a snake charmer's spell. Terrifying. Fascinating. She wants to get out, but her nipples betray her. They jut out, hard and throbbing. What's the matter with this body? All of it betrays her. A warm flush rises from between her legs, and she feels herself going wet. And welcoming. As he hands her a big wineglass full of champagne, his other hand slips between her thighs and starts kneading her.

She giggles as the wine fizzes in her mouth and warms her head. He is parting her, pressing her, letting her feel the thickness and heft of his member.

He is murmuring words in her ear, some dirty, some sappy, some filthy-sweet. And she is responding with all the nerve endings of this ripe woman's body.

With a jarring shock, the action is interrupted.

"What's the matter, hun?" the man is burbling, trying to hold her down so he can get his thing into her.

Is it an earthquake? Or a bomb?

She hears a sound like an elevator crashing inside its shaft as the whole room vibrates. A scream rattles the windows.

She feels herself being pulled backward by an unseen but irresistible force, something like a Chinese wind dragon.

She is back in her room at home, and her pubescent, flat-chested body. She studies herself in the mirror on the dresser, and experiments with stuffing cotton wool into her trainer bra. Examining the results, she's not sure she'll ever get to be the size of the woman in the hotel room. Who would want to be that size, anyway? It might give you curvature of the spine. She remembers the effect of her endowments on the man and his thing, and is smiling a secret smile when she takes her place at the dinner table.

Her elder brother sniffs her and makes a face. "Phew! Have you been eating fish?"

"Ugh," her younger brother contributes. "She's been drinking wine."

She chooses not to respond, but her mother is worried. She smells something different too.

"I spilled something in art class," Beth improvises and excuses herself to go to the bathroom.

When she comes back, her mother observes that there is "something different" about her. The boys snigger and Beth turns bright red.

"Still looks like Daddy's little girl," her father grunts round the edge of his newspaper.

Twenty years pass. After marriage and divorce, Beth is a single career woman who works hard and plays hard. She is taking a long weekend at a casino resort with her latest boyfriend, Harry. She enjoys the fact that he's always ready for her as soon as she takes off her bra. They've had one session in bed—and the sheets smell of it—and she has come from the shower, ready for champagne and a return match.

Harry is actively engaged in foreplay when she is startled to see a vortex open in midair. She looks into it, and sees far away, as if at the end of a long tunnel, a child's room with dolls and pinups and Disney toys. It's like looking into a doll's house. She is fascinated by this oddly familiar scene. There is a sad little girl, looking wistfully at her. She feels so sorry for that sad little wallflower.

She vaguely remembers a dream from her childhood, in which she came into the body of an older woman—a body as generously rounded as the one she inhabits now—and how that dream gave her the thrilling sense of a secret life until it began to fade.

"It's all right, honey. You can come in," she calls to the sad shy girl.

Harry takes this as a signal to come inside, and is pushing eagerly between her thighs.

She feels a stir of emotions, including something close to panic. When she tries to push Harry away, he thinks she is teasing him and pushes harder, trying to shove himself into her.

She opens her lungs and her scream rattles the windows.

"What the fuck?" demands Harry, not without reason, as she squirms beneath him, hitting him where it hurts.

Her heart is beating as if it is going to burst through her ribs.

The vortex is still open, a portal in space. She has to go back, to where she is safe. She lets herself flow with the motion, back to the little room up under the eaves with Minnie Mouse on a miniature rocker.

There is something terribly wrong, far more terrible than when she felt her body had never been opened, and wasn't ready.

She looks back and sees a big, full-breasted woman writhing on the bed while a hairy man holds her down, his hand over her mouth, laughing because they have done this dozens of times "and I know you love it."

She does not understand how wrong is wrong until the vortex closes. In the stillness of the slightly stale air, she runs her hands over her thin shanks and flat chest, and knows Mom is cooking meatloaf and Dad is reading the Post at the table.

She climbs into her narrow bed and pulls the covers over her head. Maybe if she shuts her eyes tight, she'll come out of this nightmare. Maybe if she goes to sleep, she'll wake up back in the hotel room with Harry.

The scene does not change. She is still trapped in the awkward, scrawny body of a thirteen-year-old.

She does not respond when they call her to the table, not until Dad comes and raps on the door.

"Phew!" says Brett, sniffing her like a dog. "Have you been eating fish?"

"Ugh," Andy contributes. "She's been drinking wine."

She is very conscious of the moistness between her thighs, and excuses herself to go to the bathroom. She washes herself, down below, and splashes cold water in her face, hoping that the pale, moony face in the mirror will change. It doesn't. She sees the movie of her life rolling forward, and she hates it. She sees herself in clothes that never fit. She sees Brett trying to climb on top of her when she finally begins to sprout, and her humiliation at the high school prom. She knows she'll flunk the wrong exams and marry the wrong man before she manages to get anything important right. She knows it will be twenty-two years before she catches up with the person who has stolen her lush grown-up body. She watches her mouth open in a silent scream.

"Don't you think there is something different about Beth?" her mother appeals to her father, who has his newspaper at the table.

"Still looks like Daddy's little girl," her father says round the edge of the Post.

UNFINISHED STORY

I'VE HAD A ROW with Fiona, in front of our guests, and the only way to deal with it is to turn my back on all that. So I am walking a Bayswater street long after midnight, hoping that the dull motion of putting one foot in front of the other will bring my blood pressure down and put me back in flow with what I was doing before things blew up. I was well under way with my new book, after all the delays and excuses and outright funks. Better than ninety pages of typescript, single-spaced. Almost enough, nearly polished enough, to send to my agent, if he is still speaking to me. It's been so long since I brought out a novel that most of my readers would be surprised by my obituary only because they might have expected to see it years ago.

I know I behaved badly after dinner, but Fiona was asking for trouble, pulling me out of my writing den to mix drinks for her socialite friends. She knows I hate to be interrupted when I'm in the zone. All I ask is to be allowed to shut the door and be left to my own devices.

Like most of our volcanic eruptions, this one started with just a hairline fissure. The hairline in question belonged to Heather Maddox Smith, Fiona's double-barreled roommate from Oxford. Since her divorce, Heather drives a little yellow sports car with a bumper sticker that reads, "I use ex-lovers for speed bumps." She is quite full of herself since she got her book published last year, and filled out her black pants suit well enough tonight to turn the heads of most of the men and a couple of the women at the party. She started off by playing the provocateur, greeting me in front of everybody with the line, "I quite fancy you, Charles"—and then adding, "but I fancy Fiona more."

When I was pouring the after-dinner drinks, Heather presumed to correct me when I delivered a favorite quotation: "Claret is a boy's drink, port is a man's, but brandy is a god's."

"No, no, Charles. Brandy is a hero's."

I knew I could not have it wrong; I've been quoting that line since I was an undergraduate. So when Heather challenged me to bet on who was right, I did not hesitate, certain that the stake—a bottle of my best cognac, or its cash value—was in my pocket. Fiona had the dictionary of quotations off the shelf before you could say Dr. Johnson. And there it was, in black and white: brandy is a hero's drink. Since I did not have a spare bottle of Delamain, I had to part with close to fifty pounds, which meant a lot more to me than it could have done to Heather, between her divorce settlement and her new job as an editor in New York, where it seems you can get away with just about anything as long as you sound like an old-school Brit.

I was very careful not to take revenge. I am old-fashioned enough to think it very bad manners to quarrel with a woman, unless you have shared a bed with her.

It was Fiona who threw the detonator. She had moved onto White Russians and was giggling with Heather on the pink sofa by the fireplace, "Charles, darling. I was just telling Heather about my dream. I dreamed the three of us were in bed together, having a fantastic time. What do you think about that?"

"I think I'll just leave the two of you to it," I said sourly.

"That's very thoughtful of you, Charles," Heather purred. "Women do have much more staying power, you know."

"Charles isn't sure about dreams," Fiona said hastily, but too late. I had to do something now.

I said to Fiona's glass, "I don't need Dr. Johnson to know a White Russian is a tart's drink. And no doubt there are dreams to match."

It is raw and cold in the street. Damp dead leaves slosh and slither underfoot, rain drizzling down the back of my neck. I button my coat at the throat. The curry palace on the corner is closed, and I have to quicken my stride to get into my usual pub in time for last orders.

The last exchange continues to trouble me, more than losing the fifty quid or having the demon Envy aroused when Heather talked about the sales figures and subsidiary rights to her book, which put my last performances in the kind of shade in which only fungus grows. The thing I can't tell either my wife or her friend is that I have also dreamed of being in bed with Heather. In my dreams, Heather is voracious. The sex is fun to begin with—she is a lovely woman, and a passionate lover—but it is relentless. She gets on top, stays on top, and finally makes me feel what it means to be screwed, in every sense of that overused word.

I am trying to shift mental gears. Maybe I can steal some material from my dreams of Heather for a steamy scene in a love-nest on the Left Bank in my next chapter. A quick pint, a walk to the park, and maybe I'll be relaxed enough to get back to the book. It's very Paris noir, perfumed by ersatz coffee and the sweat of desperate bodies coupling under the terror of the Nazi occupation. I have used smells to take me into my hero's very active love life, placing a dish of runny

Camembert next to my keyboard, puffing away at Gauloises I would not otherwise touch. Why not dip into the dreams? If I am lucky, I can get up the stairs to my study without attracting attention, and avoid Fiona until the cocktail hourtomorrow.

A dark-skinned man in an odd kind of woven skullcap, not one of our regulars, watches me finish my pint. He's close behind me as I come into the street, and I'm wary because London is not what it used to be. He could be from the Middle East, or the subcontinent, but likely as not was born in Clapham or Walthamstow. He shadows me as I head towards Kensington Gardens. The street is almost deserted, and I am not sure I want to go into the park with him on my tail. I continue walking at a steady pace, hoping that he'll forsake me for the tube station that is just ahead. He doesn't. I abandon thoughts of the park and cross the street, turning back towards Westbourne Park Road.

He crosses after me, making no effort to conceal the fact that he is following me. My inner alarm system is screaming now. I see a cab with its light on and wave it down. The cabbie's response is to turn off his light; he's had enough tips for the day.

I decide that whatever is coming after me, I had better face it head on.

When I turn round, skullcap starts speaking volubly, waving a book at me. I can't understand a word, and I am concerned that his book may be the Koran or the gospel according to the ayatollahs, though I have never heard of Islamist crazies frequenting English pubs.

I shrug and say "Inshallah," my one word of Arabic, with a little wave. I quicken my stride and when I look back, he is frozen in place, looking a little crestfallen. Whatever this is about, I am not going to let it divert me.

As I walk, I re-enter the scene I was writing when the doorbell starting ringing. A beautiful woman called Avril is drawing my hero, Mark Alter, down a long flight of stone steps. The steps end at a sheer drop, above the river far below. He is scared to take the plunge. He feels her hand on his back, encouraging.

Arhhh. How can that touch be so painful? It bursts like a hand grenade, which is not in the scene. There is a second explosion of pain, and I am falling, with him, into the golden river. The water smacks me like concrete pavement. I sink into wetness, down and down. I can't breathe. It feels like someone is tearing my heart out of my chest.

The pain blurs as everything spins and shifts. What's this? I see myself bare-bottomed on a lambskin, gurgling as grown-ups tickle my dimples. I see myself getting ready to have sex for the first time, nervous I'll lose it as I struggle to put on the rubber. I see the huge plume of smoke rising from the towers in Manhattan where I would have been had I not overslept for no obvious reason. My God, it's the worst cliché but it's true. I am watching my whole life pass before my eyes. I can't write that, can I?

It's a story, I remind myself. I am struggling to get out of it, to come up out of that river, to separate myself from my hero's disasters. Where is the woman, his lovely guide? I glimpse her red-gold hair and rush after its promise of warmth and beauty. I can breathe just fine now, and the pain is a fading memory. I look back and see a body crumpled on a darkened street. A second figure is stooped over it, ripping at the ultrasuede jacket, groping inside. The jacket is familiar. So is the odd woven skullcap.

Why me?

I have no doubt the bastard did it. There is the flash of metal in his hand, a knife or maybe a small pistol. I would hardly be anyone's idea of a significant target, but I did write a thriller years ago in which the bad guys included Arab terrorists.

I am not at all happy about the scene in the street.

I go for Skullcap with feet and fists, but my blows pass through him. He has become ghostly, a thing of congealed air. He is running away, back toward the tube station. But I see I misjudged him, twice over. He's trying to get help, yelling and waving his arms. I see now that the book he is holding is a translation of one of my old novels, with my face—still dark-haired—on the back, and that the metal object in his hand is a ballpoint pen. An autograph hound. I am almost flattered.

A police car pulls up. In no time: radio calls, an ambulance, and frantic efforts at CPR in the back on the way to the hospital.

As the scene plays out, I find I am increasingly detached from it. My writer's mind is working, working. It's a good scene: a man drops dead, doesn't know to begin with that he's dead—or how he died—and very slowly awakens to how things are after he recognizes his own body in the street. But of course it's been done to death, even in popular movies.

I am really more interested in the story I was writing before I was interrupted. It can't really have been me, on that stretcher, just a scenario playing out in my mind. A false trail. I usually get lured down a few of them before I get a book done.

I do not have time for any more interruptions.

Filled with resolve, I march back to the house. I can't seem to get the key in the door, which is a definite drawback. But I soon learn that in my present condition, doors can't stop me. I pass a foot, then an arm through the carved oak. As I pass my head through the door, I feel the molecular structure of the door stretching like toffee, shredding and rearranging. There is definite resistance. It takes a few moments to get through.

I go up the stairs to my study. The pages of the new typescript are laid out on my big partner's desk. The computer is still on. The screensaver displays a bullet train about to take off from the Gare du Nord.

I have a bright idea for how to work in some of the things that have just happened to deepen my story and bring it to an amazing conclusion that will jolt the reader out of his or her seat. I hit the space bar to return the computer to the Word program. My finger does not stop at the space bar; it goes on down through the keyboard and the surface of the desk.

The next instant, I feel myself falling gently through the bottom of the swivel chair.

I jump up. My feet seem to be sinking through the rug. My God, is all of me—whatever I am—going to fall through the floor?

Calm down, I tell myself. Maybe things will stabilize. Gingerly, I try sitting on the desk seat again. I seem to be okay, though I notice—when I inspect the situation more closely—that my rear end is not flush with the seat cushion below it. There's a perceptible space between them.

Further reality exploration will have to wait. I have a story to finish. I try the space bar again, tapping more lightly this time. Nothing happens. I hit the Enter button. I am still looking at the Gare du Nord. Maybe I'm going at it the wrong way. My energy body—if that's the right name for what I am now sitting in—may not be able to work the keys, but surely the force of my intention can influence what happens on the screen. A medium composed of electronic blips should respond to the electric force of will and desire, shouldn't it?

I focus my intention on changing the image on the screen. Bingo! We have finally left the station and are ready to shape something new. Dammit! The screen suddenly goes black and a little box appears: You have performed an illegal operation. There is an "OK" button I don't bother to try pressing.

Frustrated, I turn my attention to the pages on the desk. Nice clean typescripts, ending halfway down page 92.

I have to get this finished. I am certain it will be my enduring legacy, the thing people will be reading a century into the future.

I have an inspiration. Maybe I can find an amanuensis—someone who will take down what I dictate. Not overt channeling, I've always found that silly or embarrassing. Something far more discreet. I just want someone to write down the rest of the book, as I compose it, and deliver the finished typescript to my agent. Nobody has to know that I left the story unfinished before something knocked me down.

While I am thinking furiously about all of this, I feel a presence in my study. It is not Fiona, or one of the guests. It is a gentle presence, filled with light. There is wisdom here, and quiet strength. I see, just for a moment, something that might be the tip of a wing. An immense white wing. Even the tip is bigger than my desk.

This is most intriguing, and in part of myself, I want to go—to lift off and fly wherever a wing like that might take me.

But my years of iron-bottomed discipline win out. I have an unfinished story, and that takes priority over everything else.

The question is: who is going to help me finish the telling?

My first choice is Nigel. We worked on Fleet Street together, and in hotel bars from Copenhagen to Tuamoto, and I know that Nigel is aching to go the distance and write a book, but will never manage it alone. The one time he mustered the courage and the cash to take a year's sabbatical from the newspaper with the intention of writing in a cottage in Ireland, he simply froze up, and came home with nothing on paper except a feature on Irish whiskies for an airline magazine.

I am not sure how to get to Nigel's place, somewhere among the new dockside developments, but I find that an A to Z is no longer required. I think intently of Nigel, and I am instantly transported—with a magnificent but fleeting view of the Thames below—to a modern pub fronting the water. Nigel has had a few, and perhaps a few more, but there is nothing unusual about that. To my great relief, he is able to see me. He goggles a bit to begin with, as if he has seen a ghost.

"Is it really you? Oh Charles, O God!" He throws himself on me, blubbering, and plies me with questions.

I am trying to explain his assignment when the florid hack next to him slaps him—not gently, on the cheek—and bellows in a frightful Strine accent, "Yer bloody seeing things, mate! Get a few more down you till you're right again."

I slap the Australian reporter back, but he is impervious. It is then that I realize that Nigel is not dreaming, but is wide awake—though heavily medicated by Scottish wine and beer—and has in fact been conducting a long-distance wake in my honor.

I am encouraged that his gates of perception appear to be open, even if the view is fogged by the booze, and I resolve to try again later. So I wait patiently until closing time, trying not to become embroiled with the dead drunks who are hanging like bats from the bar, trying to get a taste through their surviving friends. Yet the atmosphere affects me, more than I had noticed in ordinary life. I feel myself becoming sodden and heavy, like a sponge filling with murky liquid.

When I accompany Nigel to his flat, I find I am not able to explain myself as well as I hoped. I watch him fall asleep. Then I see his exact double rise a foot or so above the body and rest there. Impatient, I call "Nigel!" And I observe a third Nigel, very similar to the others except lighter and more agile, separate from the floating double. Is this what goes on in dreaming? I see now that I might have done well to pay more attention when I had use of a physical body.

Nigel is once again delighted to see me, and wants to go "down the boozer" to celebrate. I am not sure this is the best environment for our purposes; I would much prefer to take him to my study and show him the typescript I want him to complete. But old habits prevail, and soon we are drinking—or experiencing a very vivid illusion of drinking—in a watering-hole that closely resembles the one where we spent the evening. When the sun rises over the East End, we both have hangovers and Nigel has no memory whatsoever of meeting me, let alone of the book project. As I watch him shave and gargle in his bathroom, I notice balefully that his sleeping attire is a T-shirt with the logo of an establishment in Amsterdam called Amnesia.

I decide that I must go to Samantha. My daughter is now twenty-two, and working as a nurse in Sydney, where I find she is living in Coogee Beach with a graphic designer who looks like a lifeguard. I am glad that once again, intention carries me the distance without need of maps, let alone air-line tickets, and I enjoy the grand vistas of continents and oceans beneath me as I fly. But the flight is taxing, even more grueling than travel cooped up in the steerage section of a jumbo jet. I arrive bleary and jet-lagged, feeling that a lot of the stuffing has been pulled out of me. At this point, I am such a novice that I have no idea about the effect of water in sucking energy out of the subtle body. Even a glass of water at the bedside can have a mildly draining effect on a phantom (a fair description of the form in which I interact with the living). There is an old superstition—with a basis in fact, like so many superstitions—that ghosts cannot cross running water. I am proof that this is not exact. However, a long ocean crossing demands a degree of stamina I had not anticipated. I feared I might be stranded in a place like Goa or Penang, where I paused for rest and recuperation, and was briefly diverted by the remarkably lively blue-light zones that operate without intermission on the astral plane.

In Coogee Beach, I find Samantha tired from her work and weepy over the news of my passing. I am touched that she has made a nightly ritual out of lighting a candle in front of my photograph and putting out a thimble of cognac and some table waters and cheese—as she did for Santa when she was a little girl.

I stroke her hair and kiss her cheek and she moves her own hands over her hair and face as if she feels me. But when I speak to her, she does not hear. And when she rises from her body in sleep, it is no better. I have become an invisible ghost to her, both in daylight and dream. I am desolated that this could be so, since we were so very close when she was small. We used to joke that, as with Athena and Zeus, the cord between us was never cut. But it is not working now. Certainly it does not transmit telephone calls.

I try phoning repeatedly after I return to England. Sometimes Samantha answers the phone and I hear her saying, "Hello? Hello?" on the other end. Once she makes my hopes soar by asking, "Daddy, is that you?" But each time our communication is swallowed by static.

I sit at my desk, mourning the unfinished typescript, while the mourning goes on around me, pooling deeper in some places than others.

Fiona is sad and angry with me, for checking out so suddenly just after we had had a tiff. I tell her it doesn't matter and hope that—although she doesn't seem to hear me—she will feel a release in her heart.

When I drop in on my old editor, Roddy Llewellyn, I find he is on the phone to Fiona, inviting himself over to the house to look at any publishable material I may have left, including the novel in progress and what he chooses to describe as "trunk books." I am greatly alarmed. If my editor sees there are 92 pages, we will not find it easy to explain the discovery of a complete new manuscript—assuming I can recruit a ghostwriter to complete it. No, not a ghostwriter. Sloppy of me to put it like that. What we require is a writer for a ghost.

I try Fiona again, urgently sending the message on the mental telegraph: Do not let Roddy into the house.

She responds by laying in a fresh bottle of Bombay Sapphire and treating herself to a facial.

I am getting weary of trying to insert myself into other people's psychic space night after night. I am considering trying to organize a series of poltergeist-type phenomena to get some attention.

My adviser—yes, I do have one, even though I am not ready to listen very closely yet—counsels that arranging physical manifestations can be highly deleterious to my evolution. But I can't see that any great harm would be done by, say, writing a message for Fiona in lipstick on her bathroom mirror or (what would certainly be easier) simply tracing one in the steam after she has taken her bath.

I have discovered there are also some rather primitive house spirits in the neighborhood who could be induced to help make a suitable demonstration. These creatures live so close to the physical plane, and can be so rowdy and obstreperous, that I am surprised I remained unaware of them when I was living in the house on Westbourne Park Road in a body of meat and bones.

Success! I have been able to make a deal with the house spirits, and they rain confusion on the day Roddy Llewellyn is due to inspect my literary oeuvre and my potentially merry widow. They cleverly arrange for her to spill red wine over the right thigh of Roddy's beautiful dove-gray Jermyn Street suit (knowing of course that Roddy dresses to the right). They cause Fiona to trip on the stairs, spraining her ankle—a minor sprain, I hasten to add, but one that requires Roddy to suspend the inspection of manuscripts in order to get my wife (sorry, widow) to an emergency room. I am now confident that we can keep up an effective barbican of resistance to literary snoops—but only for a finite time.

And it soon appears that Roddy is not the only person eager to get a look at what the poor dead writer might have left in bankable form. I am not quite in the situation of an artist whose works soar in value the moment it is known that there will not be any more of them. But the minor flurry of media attention to my life and work—even the rather rude color piece in the News of the Screws, making shameless allegations about the personal experiences that might have been the background for my spy thriller Honey Trap—has revived public interest. There is talk of doing a spiffy new boxed set of trade paperbacks. Strangest of all, the Shiraz Sayr—an obscure circle of mostly émigré Iranian intellectuals to which Skullcap belonged—is keenly interested in whether I have bequeathed a master work that will be the key to all the others. For reasons incomprehensible to me, this group of mystical beards seem to believe that my potboilers contain the code for a Gnostic journey to some fount of wisdom.

In short, something must be done soon!

So I continue to wander through the dreamscapes and the waking environments of people who might be sympathetic channels. And to sit up at all hours—since sleep is an option but not a requirement for me—working the phones.

Automatically, I dial Fiona's number, expecting nothing except static or a distant groan. I am amazed to hear a clear female voice responding.

"Who is speaking, please?"

"Fiona, this is Charles."

A shocked pause on the end of the line.

"Charles, is that really you?"

"Fiona?"

"Charles, it's Heather. I don't think Fiona is available just now. Can I give her a message?"

"Heather?" She is, of course, the last person in my social galaxy I would have considered calling. But I am growing desperate. Earlier that day, I observed two men who might have been Skullcap's brothers staking out the block. I also spotted a reporter talking to Mrs. Plum, the crazy woman next door. We have had our skirmishes, over Mrs. Plum's penchant for kidnapping any unneutered cat unfortunate enough to encounter her on the street in order to have it snipped or spayed, which makes me twinge when I think about it even in my present somewhat attenuated form. I have no doubt Mrs. Plum will contribute some more local color.

I am not sure whether it is Heather Maddox Smith or I who is more astonished when I say to her, "Have you ever considered writing a novel?"

Heather screwed me, of course. Just as I had dreamed. She stole my book. She took down everything I gave her, but then spun it around and turned it inside out, promoting a minor female character—the one who most resembled herself—to the heroine of the tale, and saddled her with the ridiculously predictable name Brigitte. My brooding Paris noir espionage classic becomes a lurid sex comedy, laced with creepy occultism. I don't know what the Shiraz Sayr will find in it, but the News of the Screws is running excerpts.

The crowning insult is that she left my name on the novel. "We owe it to poor Charles, and his readers. And who knows what further literary treasures may be discovered among his papers?"

I don't mind that Heather and Fiona are splitting the money. That's fair enough. I do mind, more than a little, that my hijacked novel is the one I will now be known by, since it has topped all the bestseller lists.

I might have handled all of this better had I done the homework that matters—by listening to my dreams and learning to go into the dreamspace where I have been living since I dropped my body. That's why Heather was the one who could receive me, of course. Whatever her silliness, she knows dreams are real.

Well, I feel my adviser pressing more strongly now, and again there is that flash of the tip of an immense white wing. My adviser resists giving me a name. I suspect this is because he finds it amusing and unevolved that I would wish to identify him as a personage separate from myself. But I know that, compared to him, I am a child, or a stumbling member of a lesser species that only yesterday crawled out of the primal soup. How did he get to be this wise, and this gentle?

He is signaling me now. You don't really want to go on repeating yourself any longer, do you?

No. If I phone Heather again, it will be a long-distance call.

FLIGHT TO DEER MOUNTAIN

BLACK WAR BIRDS in a deceptive sky, soft and blue as a baby blanket. Hard men in skins and half-armor, hacking and creaking on a steep green hillside, under dark trees.

Who am I in this place? My body is leaner and smaller. I glimpse black feathers, floating from my shoulders like man-sized wings. I cannot look more closely, because the man panting toward me is going to kill me, if he can.

He may do it with his stink. He is rank as a sweating, muddy pig. His beard is a wet haystack. A large, clumsy cross hangs on a thong from his ruddy neck.

The cross swings at my face as he cuts and slashes with his great killing iron. I am sure this Northman does not believe in the cross. It is the mark of those who have hired him, and the God whose will they claim to serve. The Northman's soul is bound to older and darker things that drink the blood of men.

My shoulder—this shoulder—aches as I parry another blow with my staff, wheeling with the ease of a dancer to avoid the massive body of the blond giant who comes rushing at me behind it. This body is quick, and seasoned, but it is tiring. And I have no weapons with which to take the offensive, except the little knife—is this a sgian dubh?—in the belt at my waist.

Get out of this now, says the voice I trust. Get away, or the pig will kill you. The battle is lost.

I take a chance. I pretend to stumble. He hurls himself back up the hill, raising his blade high for the butcher's chop. He means to take my head. Rolling past his blow with my knife in my fist, I slice his calf to the bone, and he comes down hard and heavy, grunting his pain.

I am running now, away from the combat. I have the odd sense that this body I am in is not boundaried and confined like the one I know best. As I race around the brow of the hill, and my black feathered cloak flies out, I almost believe I can lift off and fly across the valley below, to safety in deeper forests. Even on the ground, my step is lighter and higher than seems possible, for this or any man.

Some impulse slows my escape. I have to look back. There is a loyalty that calls me—not me, but the man I am in. I can feel, more than hear, a name repeating in his brain. The syllables are thick and indistinct, like something stirring in a porridge. When they start to coalesce into a word I can seize on, it is more like a girl's name than a man's. Gwendolleu. What is that?

It is the king, says the voice I know.

I remember now, or perhaps I am tapping into his memory banks, in the hippocampus or wherever they may be in an ancient brain. Gwendolleu is not a wise or generous king, but he is a king in an age that needs kings, and this man—the one that I am and am not—is his seer.

I am the King's Dolmen, his gateway to the Otherworld.

I look for Gwendolleu on the field. I know him by his blue cloak, and the dull band of metal that weighs heavy on his brow. He stands against a pack of huge northern warriors, snapping like dire wolves.

The king is dead, says the voice I know. Save what must be saved, what lives and can be reborn through you.

As the king falls under their swords, their priests are searching for the man in the raven cloak. "Diabolus!" one screams, sighting me across the hillside. Many of them are coming for me now, coming to hunt the devil.

I am running again, faster than a man is made to run. I can't look down, but if I did, it would not surprise me to see racing hooves instead of feet. I slip between the trees and leap over a stony creekbed. Up another hill, finding a trail no man's feet have made. I am running, running, through the dappled woods into the ink-dark forest, through the great trees and the cold mountain brooks to the mountain where the Deer is strong.

I rest under a ledge of rock, screened by branches from the darkening world, by the warm red waters of the chalybeate spring.

I am too warm here, inside the feathered cloak, and I unclasp it from my shoulders and fold it carefully to make a bed.

Why am I here?

I make fire with his hands, twirling sticks in a way I might have learned to do—but never mastered—in the Boy Scouts. It is his mind, as well as his fingers, that remove objects from a pouch at his belt: a sprig with dried gray-blue berries, acorns, and dried herbs. In a little metal cone, he makes incense from these ingredients. The aroma is quite pleasant. It reminds me, oddly, of sipping a gin martini in an Italian restaurant.

He is blowing the smoke across the bubbling waters.

It opens a place in which to see. Looking through his eyes, sharing his mind, I see over the paths of his life, those that are set and those that may change. I have been called here, I now know, to share in the raw terror of his times, and to understand what it took to survive.

I am to understand, in particular, why he did not become the sacrifice and that, in refusing, he did not betray his people and their cause.

The soaring, skirling power of the awen rises from his throat, and I give voice with him. I must do this, in my own time, to maintain and renew the connection with him.

There are gifts he has shared with me, some through the bloodlines, some through direct transfer across time. There will be more, but a heavy exchange will be required of me, and that will sustain him in his own world.

His hands fold us in the raven wings. We are flying now, through the smoke, back to the hill of battle, to rescue the dead king from the ghost self who is still killing and hacking.

THE THREEFOLD DEATH OF SILVER WOLF

AFTER AN EARLY FLIGHT, a long day of teaching and a jolly dinner, I am glad to settle in to the guest bedroom in the rambling frame house my friend has turned into a cozy retreat center. It's quiet here, on wooded land, near a town with one of those wonderful Midwestern names: Strongsville, Ohio. I hear only the low murmur of the Rocky River, beyond the rise where there is said to be a ring of ancient stones used by the Iroquois for sacred ceremonies.

Soon I am wandering through the courtyards of dreaming. I am startled awake by a loud burst of laughter. Blurry, I look at the bedside clock. 3:00 AM. I strain to identify the source of the noise. There are many voices, coming from the sitting room downstairs. Are there intruders? I'm quite sure my host would not be holding a loud party in the middle of the night.

I pull on shirt and jeans and pad downstairs. There is indeed a party in full swing. The party-goers are quite elegantly dressed. A tall, lean man detaches himself from a group around the baby grand piano to welcome me.

"Who are you people?" I demand.

He says clearly and distinctly, "Autochthons. We are autochthons."

I recognize the Greek and try to recall the exact meaning. His keen dark eyes wait for my recognition. There is something anomalous here, stranger than the party itself. What is it? His hair is silver. It does not stop at the hairline, it covers the whole face, darkening around the muzzle. I am looking into the face of a wolf, atop the body of a man. The wolf head is not a mask.

Shocked, I tumble out of an inner court of the dreaming, rushing through outer courts that leave no mark on memory, back into the body that did not leave the bed.

Over morning coffee, I tell my host what happened during the night. She says, "I'm sorry I missed the party. Who did the alpha male say they were, again?"

"Autochthon. It comes from the Greek." My Greek is a shambles, but the meaning is with me now. "It literally means 'sprung from the earth; aboriginal, indigenous.'"

The wolf man has told me, in the language of a Western scholar, that he and his kin are of the first peoples of this land.

I need no persuading that this is the morning to go up on the rise behind the house and investigate the ancient circle of stones among the pines and birches. The sun is shining brightly as I walk with my friend up the winding trail. When we reach the stones, she lets me go alone between two boulders. I touch them lightly, and feel at once that one of them is an archive stone, holding the memories of the land across eons.

When I pass beyond the gateway stones, I freeze, because I am not alone within the circle. The Wolf People are all around me. Their faces are now human, but they wear wolf pelts over buckskins and broadcloth. The alpha has the head of a silver wolf lolling over his own.

In bright sunlight, these people are quite substantial. Their bodies are just slightly translucent. I can see the flash of reflected light on the river through the alpha's massive form, but he is more real to me than my friend, who waits respectfully outside the stone circle. Silver Wolf, I now call him, as he communicates with me, mind to mind:

I am of the Wolf People. I am their dreamer and I guide them on the roads of this world and the Real World. We have come to you because you dream as we do, and you walk on our paths.

You wish to know the soul, and what happens to soul after the body is left behind. I now invite you to enter my death, and know the truth about these things by living and dying as I have done.

I am excited, and terrified. In the Ohio sunlight, I am about to fall into a different world. It does not occur to me to dismiss Silver Wolf and his people as figures of fantasy or hallucination. They are real, and the offer is real.

As soon as he receives my acceptance, Silver Wolf transports me into his experience of death, and life after death. I am inside his consciousness as his body is laid under the blanket of Mother Earth. And soon I am groaning and dry-heaving, because I have been buried alive. A heavy stone has been laid on my chest to prevent me from rising up. I know that what I am sharing is not the death of the physical body, but the deliberate confinement of an energy body that survives death. This is a husk that must be given to the earth and kept away from the living. I will myself to leave this energy husk in the ground, to let it suffocate and start to decompose.

Now I am above the ground, levitating and then flying. The sense of freedom is exhilarating. I can travel anywhere I want, according to my desire and imagination. I can indulge my passions and appetites. I can revisit old friends and old places, and travel to new ones. I enjoy myself like this for a time, then my astral ramblings begin to pall. I choose to rest now inside a tree, in the sleep of the heartwood.

In a few Ohio minutes, I seem to rest here for years or centuries. Then I rouse, ready for new life. I am drawn to a scene of passion, of a couple engaged in the sexual act. I stream between them, into the womb of the mother. I see myself now, from a witness perspective, as a newborn, pink and small enough to fit inside a parent's palm. This part of me has been reborn as a bear cub.

Who is the I that is watching? I am spirit, I am mind. I can return to a home among the stars. But I—as Silver Wolf—am one of those chosen to stay close to the land and watch over the earth and those who share life upon it. I will visit them in their dreams, and I will call their dream souls to me, to remind them of essential things that humans must know but are forever forgetting.

It is enough. My heart thumps as I return to the self that is standing in the circle of stones.

My friend is still waiting beyond the portal stones. "Did you feel anything?" she asks. "Was this really a place of power for Native Americans?"

"Yes," I tell her. "You could say that."

THE OTHER, AGAIN

IT HAS HAPPENED AGAIN. When this first occurred, I resolved not to write about it or think about it, for fear of losing my mind. Now that it has happened again, on January 20, 2010, I know I must write myself through it. I shall write it as a story others may read in the hope that with time I, too, will be able to read and remember it only as a story.

There was still a rheum of dirty snow about the leafless trees in the park, and ice on the paths, but I found it mild enough to sit on a bench near the lake house and contemplate the frozen pond. My little dog lay at my feet. For a few moments, the city around me was still, with an air of anticipation, like someone holding his breath. I had seen no one in the park, and was mildly irritated when a man sat down on the other end of the bench. My dog wagged his stub, but he is loose with strangers. I glanced at the newcomer out of the corner of my eye. He was very young, with long dark hair falling over his shoulders from under an absurdly romantic beret. No doubt one of the transient college kids who come and go in my neighborhood, or one of the hungry artists who hang their pictures for a week at a time in the transient basement galleries.

He made an awkward ritual out of stuffing and lighting a cherrywood pipe. The heavy fruited scent of his tobacco carried me back across time, to an awkward young man I had once known well.

I turned to him and asked if he was smoking Amphora tobacco.

Without meeting my eyes, he agreed that he was.

I inspected him more closely, the wide shoulders and narrow body, the silk scarf at his throat, the maroon-colored journal book, big as a child's tombstone, in his hand.

"Then I know who you are," I told him. "You are Robert Moss, though you sign your articles and poems R. J. Moss in The Canberra Times and the student paper."

-He returned my inspection. "I know you from somewhere. Are you one of Dad's brothers?"

"I am Robert Moss. I am you. I've just lived a lot longer."

"You're crazy."

"What year do you think it is?"

"It's 1965, of course."

"You are mistaken. Today is Wednesday, January 20, 2010."

"Don't come the raw prawn with me! It's bloody 1965."

-I was tickled by the way that, when rattled, he became a bit more of an Aussie than was his natural style. "Then you are living in Bruce Hall on the campus of the Australian National University. In your bookcase you have Baudelaire's Fleurs du Mal and Dante's Inferno in Italian—but not the rest of the Commedia, because you have not yet found the comedy in life—and the Penguin editions of Dostoyevsky, Faulkner, and Homer. You also have a blue-bound copy of Kautilya's Arthashastra, which fascinates and repels you because it teaches that the law of life is 'Big fish eat little fish.'"

R. J. Moss was not impressed. "Of course you know what books I have in my room. I'm dreaming, and you're a part of me that for some reason is appearing as an old man with white hair who's been eating rather well. So you know what I know."

"Did you know that the man who loaned you the Arthashastra will become your father-in-law?"

As he stared at me, I added, "You haven't met his daughter yet, but you will, when she comes out from England. She'll get a job in a bookshop, your natural hunting ground. On the day you first speak to her she'll be helping a customer who wants to purchase a map of the world that does not include the United States."

"You are one of my thought forms, and you will disappear if I tell you to."

"You got that from one of your books on magic, probably Dion Fortune. Try it if you like. It won't do you any good."

"You claim I am going to marry my professor's daughter."

"Yes, but it won't last. You will marry much too young, with too much of life ahead of you to stay in a nest. Anyway, for a while you'll be seized with a reckless desire to fight battles. You'll get over it, but not until you've been bloodied. Then you'll marry again. You'll notice the woman who will become your second wife when she tells you she can dream the result of a horse race."

"This is definitely a dream."

"Where do you think you are now?"

"I'm sitting at the edge of the lake in Canberra, and it's bloody hot. That silly water jet doesn't make things any better."

He made the motion of fanning his face. I recalled that in that absurdly oversized book he lugged everywhere with him, he had drawn a picture of Nietzsche at the edge of madness, and written an interminable series of poems for a girl, now lost, he called Lady of Khorasan, even though she had bad teeth and had never been outside New South Wales, except to study in the dreary capital, set down in the bush at an airless remove from the ocean beaches that are the country's lungs.

At this age, he lived for poetry, I remembered. Perhaps I could move him with a line he had not yet encountered, more than with a preview of his future that, while factual, seemed to him full of impossibilities.

"I will say something you do not know but whose reality you will accept because it is poetic truth. Are you willing to hear?"

He nodded.

"Il faut vivre comme un ours."

He frowned a little. "'One has to live like a bear?' Is that right?"

My turn to nod.

"Who said that?"

"Flaubert."

"Not possible."

"You haven't read enough Flaubert to know. And you have yet to write a novel. You will write novels, and will publish many. More important, you will meet the Bear and this will change everything." My tone indicated that we were no longer talking about any bear, but the Bear. "You won't understand until he comes for you, and that will be in North America, when you are twice your present age."

"This is the strangest dream. I don't believe I'll remember any of it. But just in case, if you have lived my life ahead of me, what can you tell me that can help me?"

-I considered telling him: you'll break hearts and your heart will be broken in turn, but you must never stop living from the heart. There is one who watches over us and never leaves us. Swim whenever you can. Listen to your dreams and move always in the direction of your dreams. Beware of a woman with razors in her eyes, and a sheriff in the Blue Ridge Mountains who makes moonshine in his bathtub. Never lose your sense of humor, once you find it again. Don't reverse your steps once you have crossed the Pont Neuf. Define yourself, as many times as necessary, to escape being defined by others.

What I said was, "Twenty-three years from now, you will be booked on an early plane to Philadelphia, with the intention of driving to a certain house in Lancaster County. You must not take that plane."

-"What's in Lancaster County?"

"Trust me on this. Will you remember?"

He shrugged. I knew he would forget, but an hour before he was due to leave for the airport, twenty years into his future, more than twenty years into my past, a dream would remind him. I knew this because—but for that dream—I would not be alive today and we could not be sitting on this bench together.

He surprised me by saying, "I have something for you: Ich bin ein Funke nur vom heilengen Feuer."

I remembered now that I—that is, he—had taken some German in order to read Rilke in the original. My German did not stick; I can barely manage to order sausages in a beer cellar.

"Rilke?"

His mouth curved into a faintly superior smile. "It seems I know things that you do not." His mood flickered like a shadow on the ice. "This is the strangest dream. I know I'll forget it. If not, you would have known we would meet this morning."

I thought of a notion of Coleridge. A man dreams he is in paradise, and he is given a flower as proof. When he wakes, he has the flower in his hand. And what then?

"Let's give each other something," I proposed. I dug in my pockets and came up with a wad of crumpled bills. I separated the least disreputable and handed it to him. He examined the face of the wigged man inside the oval, and lingered over the occultists' pyramid on the back with the eye in its floating apex. I drew his attention to the small text next to the signature of the Secretary of the Treasury: "SERIES 2006."

He groped in his own pockets in turn and produced a gum nut.

"Look at the time," he jumped up. "I must be going."

As he rose, my little dog jumped up too, wagging his stub.

-"There's one thing more," I said. "Dogs love you no matter what."

-"I know."

-We did not shake hands or have body contact in any way. We walked away from each other in opposite directions. I did not look back; I cannot say whether he did.

One day after this encounter, I cannot find the gum nut I put in the breast pocket of my shirt, which I threw in the laundry hamper at the end of the day and only searched this morning. When I walked my dog today, I made a point of not returning to the bench by the lake.

But something is still in play because I noticed that the big maroon journal—his journal, from 1965—has surfaced in the room I use as my archive. It was clearly visible near the top of a stack of notebooks in an open documents box. Of course I had to pull it out. I treated it as I do any book, opening it at random to see what comes up.

The book of R. J. Moss fell open at pages numbered 114 and 115 in his hand. The bottom half of page 115 was filled by his drawing of Nietzsche staring into the pit of madness. The upper half of page 114 contained his copy of a word-picture of Stefan George by André Gide, in French. Below this, in script running diagonally across the page, giving the general impression of a wing, R. J. Moss inscribed several verses of Stefan George, including the line "Ich bin ein Funke nur vom heiligen Feuer" with the translation, "I am a spark of the holy fire."*

---

*Jorge Luis Borges' story "The Other" came to me twice, in mysterious ways, over the holiday season in 2009-2010. Just before Christmas, I woke with the certain knowledge that there was something by Borges that I had not read that I needed to find that day. I have many editions of Borges on my shelves (I've been reading him since 1970), but I went to my nearby magic bookshop at opening time to see if anything popped up. There, atop a pile of new arrivals, was a translation of Borges' late collection *The Book of Sand*. The opening story is "The Other," in which Borges, seated on a bench beside the Charles River in Cambridge, Massachusetts, in 1969, encounters a young man who proves to be his own younger self, who thinks he is sitting by the lake in Geneva in 1919 and is reluctant to believe this encounter can be other than a dream. Borges gets the attention—and wins the partial belief—of his younger self by reciting an amazing line of Victor Hugo that the young man has not yet discovered, about the "hydra-universe" twisting its "scales of stars."

Then early in January, ranging around in the early hours in the midst of leading a workshop, I opened a 500-page edition of Borges' *Collected Fictions*, in Andrew Hurley's excellent translation, as a random act of bibliomancy, and found myself at the first page of "The Other," again.

Like Borges, I am intrigued by the possibility—for me, a certainty—that we can meet our past and future selves. In homage to the great Argentine writer, I have borrowed the outline of his story, just as he borrowed the ideas and the form of a story by Kurd Lasswitz (which he reviewed in an essay titled "The Total Library") to craft his celebrated "Library of Babel."

THE JOURNEY TO ABSOLUTE KNOWLEDGE

TRAVELERS ARE PREPARING for the journey into the desert, beyond the maps, beyond the cities and the last outposts of consciousness. There are many roads that lead away from Absolute Knowledge, only a few that will bring the traveler to a true point of entry.

The great scholar-city of Anamnesis is devoted to opening the ways, and some fly directly from its towers toward the great shining disk that is the portico of the Absolute. Elaborate maps are drawn up and plans produced showing the revolutions of the stars and the star-beings who guard the gates of the ascent to the highest knowledge. Yet some of the brilliant scholars here mistake their maps for the journey, and are lost in their studies when the call comes to take the road.

Some find their ways through the Dreamlands. Many more have become lost or entangled, and return through the parched lands where dying dreams gasp or flounder like fish beached on a shore.

Few who stumble into the Souqs of Hearsay—where travelers' tales and talismans are traded, and dubious guides tout their services—find their way.

In the canebrakes of Half-Remembered Things, thoughts and visions take flight like waterfowl. Most escape. Some are brought down, stone dead, by careless hunters. Only the hunter with a subtle net can bring them home. We can be diverted for whole lifetimes from the journey in the closed Cities of Revelation, where people are penned within received and fixed beliefs. From some of the closed cities, no legal exit is permitted; to continue the journey you must make an escape—and risk terrible punishments if you are caught.

In the Swamps of Forgetting and the Zona Rosa, caught in the wallows of addiction, no one recalls the existence of a zone of Absolute Knowledge. In the Cities of the Reducers, ruled by scientific materialism, the possibility of higher dimensions is denied and dreamers conceal their dreams for fear of being confined to mental institutions.

I discuss arrangements for a journey to Absolute Knowledge with a pleasant couple. The woman has worked with me for a long time and has traveled through many mythic gates. Her husband is tall and lean, with glasses. He is diffident about his readiness to join our expedition. I share a vision in which he is playing a key role as our quartermaster, thanks to the immense resources he will soon inherit from his mother, a fierce matriarch and mistress of a commercial empire—sending ships and tankers across the seas—who also has a deep interest in esoteric things.

We are gathering horses, equipment, provisions. I tie and retie a curious pair of black sandals whose front straps are loose. The diffident man astonishes us by driving incredibly fast through narrow spaces in a busy shopping district, pulling with remarkable skill through a space only an inch or so wider than his vehicle.

Who returns from the journey to Absolute Knowledge? Where can we find them and consult with them?

Can the blind Ute woman really be one of those who have made the journey?

Can the silent old man who sits all day among animals—stray cats and dogs and others—be one of the successful voyagers?

My expedition is almost complete. I am discussing the final arrangements—including such technical questions as whether we will require camels as well as horses for the desert crossing—with the couple who are devoted to my work.

The entrance to the realm we are seeking appears as a desert of clean, striated white sand, edged by a few palms and the last oasis.

There can be no turning back, after this.

ACKNOWLEDGMENTS

I am grateful to all those creative spirits who shared the adventures that gave birth to the poems and stories in this collection, and were often the first to hear them, in gatherings by the fire on a mountain in the Adirondacks, or under the skylight of a great yurt in the mossy woods in the foothills of the Cascades, or above the rocky beach where fresh water joins salt water at Big Sur, California, or in the Midi in France, close to wild boars and black bulls and strange, shifting winds. The first drafts of many of the poems collected here were written to fulfill the creative homeplay assignments I suggest to members of my depth workshops and trainings, which include my five-residential retreat, "Writing as a State of Conscious Dreaming."

I thank two of my other publishers for permission to include here several poems that appeared in previous books:

"The Return Journey" appeared in *Dreaming the Soul Back Home* by Robert Moss, published by New World Library (2012). All rights reserved.

"Bear Giver," "Eyes of the Goddess," and "Birth of Apollo" appeared in *Dreamways of the Iroquois* by Robert Moss, published by Destiny Books, a division of Inner Traditions International (2005). All rights reserved.

A big mahalo to Caren Lobel-Fried for permission to use her wonderful image of Pele dreaming on the cover, and for much instruction on the language and many modes of Hawaiian dreaming, especially through her book Hawaiian Legends of Dreams.

I am grateful to James Peltz and the wonderful people at State University of New York Press for bringing this first collection of my poems and stories to the world.

ABOUT THE AUTHOR

Robert Moss is a novelist, poet and independent scholar and the creator of Active Dreaming, an original synthesis of dreamwork and shamanism. Born in Australia, he survived three early near-death experiences, found himself "at home in the multiverse" and started writing poetry from there when very young.

In midlife, on a farm in the Hudson Valley of New York, his visionary encounters with an ancient Mohawk woman shaman led him to follow a path for which there is no career track in our culture, that of a dream teacher.

He leads creative and shamanic adventures all over the world, including "Writing as a State of Conscious Dreaming" and a three-year training for teachers of Active Dreaming. His many nonfiction books include *Conscious Dreaming, Dreamways of the Iroquois, The Secret History of Dreaming, Dreamgates,* and *Dreaming the Soul Back Home.* His novels include the three volumes in the Cycle of the Iroquois—*Fire Along the Sky, The Firekeeper* and *The Interpreter*—also published by Excelsior Editions. Moss lives with his family in upstate New York. His website is www.mossdreams.com. One of his rules for everyday living: "Commit poetry every day, in every way."